NEW YORK TIMES BESTSELLING AUTHOR

TARA JANZEN

CRAZY HEARTS

"Bad boys are hot, and they don't come any hotter than the Steele Street gang..."
—*Romantic Times*

MISSION TWELVE

A STEELE STREET NOVELLA PLUS PANAMA JACK

CRAZY HEARTS
Steele Street, Mission 12
Copyright © 2020 by Tara Janzen

All rights reserved. Except for use in any review, the reproduction or utilization of this work in whole or in part in any form by any electronic, mechanical or other means, now known or hereinafter invented, including xerography, photocopying and recording, or in any information storage or retrieval system, is forbidden without the written permission of the publisher.

This is a work of fiction. Names, characters, places and incidents are either the product of the author's imagination or are used fictitiously, and any resemblance to actual persons, living or dead, business establishments, events or locales is entirely coincidental.

Printed in the USA.

Cover Design and Interior Format
© THE KILLION GROUP, INC.

PRAISE FOR THE NOVELS OF TARA JANZEN

CRAZY COOL
"Wild nonstop action, an interesting subplot, a Tormented-but-honorable and brilliant bad boy and a tough girl, and great sex scenes make Janzen's…romance irresistible." —*Booklist*

CRAZY KISSES
"Sultry sex, harrowing adventure, fantastic characters, what more could you ask for?" —*Fresh Fiction*

"The high-action plot, the savage-but-tender hero, and the wonderfully sensual sex scenes, Janzen's trademarks, make this as much fun as the prior Crazy titles."—*Booklist*

CUTTING LOOSE
"Bad boys are hot, and they don't come any hotter than the Steele Street gang…This novel is smoking in the extreme!"
—*Romantic Times*

"A non-stop thrill ride…Don't miss CUTTING LOOSE."
—*Romance Reviews Today*

LOOSE AND EASY
"Sexual tension crackles and snaps…Crossing and double-crossing is on most of the characters' agendas which keeps the pace fast and the action sharp… Janzen's place in the romantic suspense pantheon is assured." *–Romantic Times*

RIVER OF EDEN
"One of *the* most breathtaking and phenomenal adventure tales to come along in years! [Tara Janzen] has created an instant adventure classic. Make tracks and get your hands on a copy of this book today! –Jill M. Smith for *RT*

THE CHALICE AND THE BLADE
"Magnificent storytelling, complex, flesh-and-blood characters. *The Chalice and the Blade* is so compelling, I read it in one sitting."
–Iris Johansen *New York Times bestselling author*

"An enthralling, exhilarating rush of a read.
– Amanda Quick *New York Times bestselling author*

TITLES BY TARA JANZEN

THE STEELE STREET NOVELS
Crazy Hot
Crazy Cool
Crazy Wild
Crazy Kisses
Crazy Love
Crazy Sweet
On the Loose
Cutting Loose
Loose and Easy
Breaking Loose
Loose Ends
Crazy Hearts

THE STAND-ALONE NOVELS
River of Eden
The Chalice Trilogy:
The Chalice and the Blade
Dream Stone
Prince of Time

CLASSIC ROMANCES, INCLUDING:
Avenging Angel
Shameless
Outlaw Carson
The Courting Cowboy

CHAPTER ONE

4th of July, 738 Steele Street, Denver, Colorado

DYLAN HART STOOD ON THE rooftop of 738 Steele Street, sipping a smooth, single malt Scotch and doing his damnedest to enjoy the sunset. It was spectacular, the craggy peaks of the Rockies backlit by a color–drenched sky streaked with clouds. Abso-fricking-lutely gorgeous – but not enough to hold his attention.

He shifted his gaze back to the city streets and the dark alley below, checking for trouble, looking for anything out of place or for anybody going against the grain. Two days back from their last mission out of Qatar, and he was still in battle mode, still on full alert, still ready and waiting for the worst of whatever happened next.

Right. Battle mode in a pair of flip-flops, board shorts, and a Hawaiian shirt. The only thing happening next was dinner.

"You're thinking too hard, boss," his teammate Christian Hawkins, a.k.a. Superman, said. "I can smell your brain burning from here."

"That's the steak you're smelling, not my brain," Dylan said, turning around to face the somewhat disconcerting sight of one of the world's most kickass operators manning a barbeque grill and wearing a baby backpack complete with a baby, a bottle, and a binky.

"Maybe it's time for you to give those rib-eyes a flip."

"They're still mooing." Christian poked the nearest steak with his finger, testing its temperature. In the backpack, the baby burbled and babbled and kicked. When one of his booties fell off, Dylan bent down to pick it up.

"Rare is good," he said, wrestling the little knitted shoe back on Hawkins's youngest, Hank. "Still mooing is even better."

At five-months old, Hank was built like an Abrams tank - an Abrams tank wearing knitted palm tree booties, a teeny Hawaiian shirt to match his dad's, and a sun hat that looked like a coconut on his head.

Geezus, Dylan thought. When had all this happened?

He looked around the rooftop at a sea of Hawaiian shirts, sarongs, orchid leis, and little kids, at tables laden with potato salad, vegetable trays, cherry pies and chocolate cake – standard operating procedure, SOP, for Steele Street's Independence Day rooftop picnic. The tradition went back to their chop shop days, when, as a bunch of bona fide juvenile delinquents, they'd grilled hotdogs on the roof and hoped to score a couple of six packs to celebrate the Fourth of July. The Hawaiian shirts had come later, fifteen-year-old Glenlivet even later, and long after the shirts and the single malt, women and children and sarongs and binkies, unimaginable in the early years, had rolled into Steele Street like a runaway train.

Life was good.

He took another sip of Scotch.

Maybe too good.

"Flip the steaks, Superman," Creed Rivera hollered from across the rooftop, lifting his beer bottle in salute with a tow-headed, blue-eyed, eighteen-month-old beauty named Olivia sitting on his shoulders, her little fingers clutching handfuls of the Jungle Boy's hair.

"Flip 'em," another of Steele Street's kickass operators, Red Dog, added her vote. Dressed in a luminous blue sarong she only looked about half as deadly as usual. The girl had mad fighting skills.

A curvaceous, buxom blonde – with no fighting skills whatsoever - crossed over to the grill and stretched up on tiptoe to kiss Christian's cheek.

"Burn one for me, babe," Katya "Bad Luck" Hawkins told her husband. Two little kids trailed in her wake. At six years old, Alexandria was the "boss of everybody." A position hotly contested by her younger brother, three-year-old Wes. Hank had yet to complain about his older sister's authoritarian streak.

And smack dab in the middle of all the action was Dylan's own little brood, one sinfully gorgeous, long-legged blonde named Skeeter chasing a two-year-old, dark-haired cherub with Dylan's independent streak and a little pair of eyebrows shaped exactly like his daddy's - Grady Hart.

As always, just looking at the two of them made Dylan's chest tighten in a slightly painful way.

That was what the good life gave a guy – heartburn. A world-class case of it.

He dug in the pocket of his board shorts and came up with a roll of antacids. Four of them went in his mouth. The rest he tucked into his shirt pocket, damn certain he'd need them all before the night was through.

He'd been home for two days and was leaving again in three. An old enemy had surfaced in Panama City, Vasily Nikolayevich, a former FSB agent turned illegal arms dealer. Dylan's boss, General Buck Grant, and a whole lot of other people in Washington, D.C. wanted to know who the Russian was dealing with and what he was selling – and if necessary, how to stop him.

All Dylan wanted was to stay home with his son and

make love to his wife, but he'd been tagged for the job.

Skeeter knew the score. She had her own place on the Special Defense Force, SDF, team, the group of black-ops shadow warriors housed at 738 Steele Street in Denver who specialized in doing the Defense Department's dirty work.

Yeah, Skeeter knew the score, but being a mother had clipped her wings a bit, and she was getting restless.

Restless women made Dylan nervous.

A restless wife gave him heartburn.

Skeeter finally caught up with bad boy Grady, a.k.a Puppy, Bubba, Sweetie-pie, and Cutie-pants, when he scrambled into the wading pool. He was in good company. His best friend, Jesse Rivera, Olivia's twin brother, was already in the water, splashing around under the watchful eye of his mother, Cody.

Honestly, there were so many kids at Steele Street these days, Dylan was losing count. Instead of SDF, he thought they should be calling themselves FERTILE.

Skeeter bent down and kissed the top of Grady's head, but before Dylan had a chance to process the lovely vision of her long legs, silky sarong, and platinum blond ponytail flowing over her shoulders, and way before he got his Top Ten Favorite Bad Girl Fantasy list fired up, it was all over. She straightened suddenly, her gaze focused to the north, and he knew something had set off her spidey-sense.

He followed her gaze, and was clueless. The Georgia O'Keefe sunset stretched north along the Front Range all the way to the horizon and the cowboy state beyond.

"Wyoming?" he asked, crossing the rooftop to stand by his wife's side.

She shook her head, her attention shifting slightly, to north by northeast, to the Great Plains and a clear blue sky. "Storm heading this way."

Always, Dylan thought, not doubting it for a second.

Behind them, a cheer went up, and they turned to see a new batch of arrivals – Travis James, Red Dog's "Angel," was in the lead with a case of local craft beer hoisted on his shoulder, behind him, Quinn and Reagan Younger were bustling their brood of four up the stairs and onto the deck.

Quinn looked like he needed a shot of something, anything...maybe two. Dylan lifted his glass and Quinn grinned, holding up 3 fingers sideways.

Yeah, Dylan understood.

Dax Killian and Suzi Toussi came next, Dax with a panatela cigar clenched between his teeth, carrying four bottles of Dom Perignon to stick in the beer cooler. Suzi had brought a bottle of Campari and a crystal bowl full of orange slices and lemon peels to the party. The girl liked her Americanos.

Dylan felt the tightness in his chest relax a bit. It was a good day. More than half the crew had made it home for the 4th.

He glanced back at Skeeter, who was still looking out toward the horizon, and he hoped to hell whatever was heading their way could hold off for today. Just one day, that's all he asked.

Another cheer went up, everyone laughing, and Skeeter turned. Dylan checked his six just in time to see all of Quinn's kids pile into the water, creating a sloppy ruckus of little heathens.

"Uh, babe," he said. "We need" - a wave of water splashed over the edge of the wading pool and soaked his flip-flops.

"A bigger pool," she finished for him, laughing.

Yeah, he thought, the toughest team of badass operators to ever come out of the Department of Defense needed a bigger wading pool.

CHAPTER TWO

4th of July, Northeastern Colorado

THREE HOURS OUT OF GRAND Island, Nebraska, racing across northeastern Colorado at 100 mph, Liam Dylan Magnuson knew he wasn't going to make it. He was going to die out here in the godawful middle of nowhere.

Tightening his hands on the steering wheel, he pressed down on the Porsche's accelerator and took the 718 Cayman up to 110 mph. He was flying through the night, the full moon rising behind him, the road stretched out flat and straight ahead of him, black asphalt and yellow stripes running under his wheels.

Every breath hurt.

His body ached.

Blood ran down the side of his face and half a dozen other places.

Nate Martell had beaten the hell out of him in Grand Island, hit him again and again, and his own damn stepbrother, Tommy Dunstan, had cut him across the arm with a damn Bowie knife, but Liam hadn't given up the name or the place they wanted so goddamn badly.

"Where you going, boy?" Tommy had demanded, shoving Liam up against the side panel of Nate's Escalade. "Who you running to? You better tell me, boy, or there'll be hell to pay."

"Ain't telling you nothing, Tommy." He'd kicked out, trying to break free, and Bobby Lee Raynor had shot him – a hot gash across the top of his thigh meant to wound, not kill, but he still hadn't given them anything, not the name of the man he was chasing down, and not the place where he hoped to hell he could find him.

Fuck you, Big Jack Dunstan.

He should have ditched the car in Iowa, when he'd figured out Big Jack's jokers had been tracking him since Chicago, but the Porsche was fast, really fast, and it had felt like his only chance. He'd been wrong, and he was paying for the mistake with every breath he took.

But the name, the name was still his to hold, the way he'd been holding onto it for his whole goddamn life. He'd never spoken it to another living person, no friend, no pillow-talk girl, and most of all, never to his mother, Momma Margot, or the corrupt southern bastard she'd married, Big Daddy Jack Dunstan.

He'd told his bandmates everything during their long nights on the tour bus driving from one gig to the next, the good and the bad of his poor-little-rich-boy life – but not the name.

The name was his to hold, close to his heart, a balm to his soul - and now, out here on the Great Plains, the death of him, if he couldn't outrun his stepbrother, Tommy, and the rest of Daddy Jack's men all the way to Denver.

He put his chances at less than even, at best.

Ahead of him, a sudden curve snaked out of the dark night. He hit it, and the Porsche skidded hard to the outside edge of the pavement, the wheels spitting up gravel, the chassis shaking. He held the car with every ounce of strength he had, foot off the gas, his hands locked onto the steering wheel, and *thank God*, the Cayman stuck to the road. A second later, he fed the beast more gas and accelerated out of the turn, not daring to slow down, no matter how fast his heart was pounding.

He was so damned lost.

Liam had thought he'd seen it all, London, Sydney, Hong Kong, New York, Chicago, L.A., but he'd never seen this much empty – 360 degrees of empty with a few lights scattered through the darkness.

The only clue he had to his location was the Colorado state highway sign he'd passed five miles back.

"California," he'd said, spitting out a mouthful of blood, when Tommy had asked him for the third time where he was going.

But he knew Tommy hadn't bought the lie.

The bastard had been chasing him down since the first time he'd bailed out of boarding school. He'd been fourteen years old, and it had taken Tommy two months to catch him down in the Florida Keys.

He didn't know why his mother and Big Daddy Jack had bothered dragging him home every time just to send him away someplace else, someplace they thought could hold him. Hell, he hadn't lasted a week in military school, and so it had gone, one school after another, until graduation, when they'd finally thrown up their hands, cut him loose, and let him go his own way.

But the game had changed when Tommy had shown up in Chicago, waving a letter from a New York City attorney about an inheritance. From that moment on, the game had gotten mean, and in Grand Island, out in the dark beyond the edges of an interstate truck stop, Tommy had taken it into the gutter.

Five million dollars could do that to a person.

A cool five million sitting on ice with Liam's name on it.

Except it wasn't his money, and the name on it, though exactly the same as his, wasn't his. It never had been. Long before he'd come along, the name had belonged to someone else, a fifteen-year-old boy who'd done a helluva lot better job escaping Momma Margot and Big Daddy Jack than Liam had managed. That boy had disappeared and taken a new name, and Liam was racing toward Denver, holding it close, determined to find him.

CHAPTER THREE

―◆―

5th of July, Denver, Colorado

LIEUTENANT LORETTA BRADLEY OF THE Denver Police Department had never seen a ghost...until today in room 320 at Denver General Hospital. The ghost, an apparently "almost famous" rock musician who had the younger nurses all aflutter, had been found in an alley north of downtown with a Porsche key and two thousand dollars in his pocket, a black leather backpack slung over his shoulder, a gunshot wound on his leg, and eerily, given his face, a knife wound across his upper left arm. She knew three special ops bad boys with knife scars on their upper left arms, and nothing about this guitar hero said he belonged in their company – except that face.

Standing by the hospital bed, looking down at the young man sleeping off a dose of painkiller, Loretta let out a long, slow breath. Nothing was ever easy – but this took the cake, the whole damn, triple layer, double Dutch chocolate cake.

Even looking straight at the boy, she found it hard to believe what she was seeing.

"Did they find the Porsche?" she asked the uniformed cop standing next to her.

"Yes, ma'am." Officer Weisman said. "Over on 60th, about half a mile from where the warehouse security guard found him in an alley."

"Impound?"

"They're picking it up now."

Loretta flipped the young man's wallet open again and stared at the Illinois driver's license – Liam Dylan Magnuson. She didn't know the name, or his stage name, Liam Magnus, almost famous or not, but she knew the face – oh, hell yeah, she knew the face - the same way she knew the address and name scrawled on the back of a business card tucked inside the wallet – *Uptown Autos, 738 Steele Street, Denver, Colorado.*

"Did you contact the Chicago police?"

"Yes, ma'am. They're checking the address on the registration and will get back to us as soon as they have something."

Loretta nodded and handed the young man's wallet back to the officer before taking out her phone. She knew the guy who could clear up the mystery, maybe the only guy who could clear it up, but after a couple of rings, all she got was Dylan Hart's voicemail.

"Good morning, Dylan, Lieutenant Loretta here. I'm at Denver General with a man named Liam Dylan Magnuson, and I'd like you to come down here to confirm his identity. We're in room 320."

Her next call went to Christian "Superman" Hawkins, Dylan's second in command at Special Defense Force, SDF.

"*Yo,* Lieutenant."

"Christian, I'm at Denver General staring at a problem named Liam Dylan Magnuson. You ever hear of him?"

"No, ma'am."

Loretta wasn't surprised. She and Dylan's crew were tight, and if she'd never heard of the guy, she figured it was a long shot that any of the SDF operators had ever heard of him either – except for Dylan Hart. She'd be surprised as hell if Dylan didn't know him.

But whether they knew him or not, every last operator on the SDF team would recognize the boy lying in the hospital bed, despite his long hair, pierced ear, and colorful tattoos.

"He also goes by the name Liam Magnus as frontman and lead vocalist for a band called Never Celeste. Any of that sound familiar?"

"No," Christian said. "Not the stage name or the band. What's up?"

"That's what I was hoping you could tell me. Can you get down here and take a look at him for me? He's... uh, he's – well, hell, just get down here *pronto*. We're in room 320."

"*Absolutamente, Jefe.* Be there in ten."

"Do us both a favor and stick to the speed limit, Superman. I'll see you in fifteen." She hung up and slipped the phone back in her pocket.

An older nurse came in to check on the patient, and Loretta and Officer Weismann stepped aside – but they didn't leave. Someone had manhandled the boy, and with that face, until Loretta had a few answers, she and Weismann were staying put. Two younger nurses came in to dawdle and gawk, one of them with an honest-to-God autograph book in her hand, which wasn't going to do the girl much good with the "almost famous rock star" still out cold – not that the young nurse seemed to mind.

Watching her, Loretta wondered if she'd ever, at any age, had such a sappily smitten expression on her face.

Maybe once, she silently admitted with a grin, thinking of the hard-assed SOB who'd stolen her heart – General Buck Grant, the man who'd created the SDF team out of a group of misfits, wild cards, and Marines.

Weisman's phone buzzed, and while he talked, Loretta let the nurses fuss and coo. But as soon as Weisman hung up, she caught the older nurse's eye with a look that had the room cleared in seconds.

"Chicago," Weisman said when they were alone again. "The address is good, a pricey lakefront condo with a view and not a family member in sight. The condo is for sale, and no one has filed a missing person report."

"What about the other band members, or a manager or something?"

"Chicago PD is trying to track them down. They'll let us know when they've got someone."

Well, hell, she thought, looking back at the boy. After a moment, she tilted her head to one side.

"Is that a Jimi Hendrix tattoo on his arm?"

"Yes, ma'am," Weisman answered. "Looks like Hendrix got the worst of it last night."

Sure enough, Loretta thought. A neat row of stitches holding the knife wound closed went directly across Jimi's face, a straight line of them beneath his eyes, giving Jimi kind of a "masked man" look. Liam Magnuson had a skull-and-crossbones tattooed over his heart, a three-inch scar, long healed, along his jaw, and a string of Latin words – *Dum vivimus, vivamus* – tattooed across his lean, six-pack abs. According to another of the young nurses who'd wandered into the room earlier, the guy also sported a really super cool bird tattoo on his back, like a crow in flight or something.

Loretta didn't doubt the super coolness of anything about this boy. Liam Dylan Magnuson exuded cool from his ninety-thousand-dollar ride and his designer leather jacket to his two hundred dollar haircut and the gold hoop in his ear. But if he thought he was a badass pirate with a Porsche, he didn't know what real badass pirates looked like.

He was about to find out.

She heard the door open behind her, and with a single glance at the man entering the room, knew the boy's life was about to change forever.

CHAPTER FOUR

—◆—

CHRISTIAN HAWKINS STOOD BY THE hospital bed and tried to come up with an explanation for what he was seeing. He glanced at Loretta and opened his mouth to say something, then didn't.

Geezus. His gaze strayed back to the young man in the bed.

Loretta had been vague on the phone, and one look at the boy told him why.

It was *déjà vu* and *what in the hell* all rolled into one. The long hair, earring, and tattoos didn't fit, but the face was a snapshot straight out of his past – Dylan Hart, SDF's commanding officer, in his early twenties.

He looked at Loretta again, but still didn't know what to say.

She shrugged in understanding. Lieutenant Loretta was a no-nonsense cop, nearly six feet of big-boned, "take names and kick butt" female with a tight bun of graying red hair coiled on top of her head, and a pair of golden brown eyes that in the right light made her darn near beautiful. Hawkins didn't have to work very hard to understand why General Grant had fallen for her.

"There are only two possible explanations," she said.

Yeah. Two.

"Either Dylan was damn busy twenty-some years ago," she continued. "Or he left a little brother behind when he reinvented himself and landed in the middle of my precinct jacking cars."

Yeah. Either one of those would explain the young man lying in the bed, Dylan's son, or Dylan's younger brother - but nothing explained why Hawkins had never heard of the guy, whoever he was. Not a word. Not in twenty-three years of watching Dylan's back like it was his own. They were closer than brothers, and now here was this kid with Dylan's face and a skull-and-crossbones tattooed on his chest.

Then it hit him – twenty-three years.

"How old is Liam?" he asked.

"According to his driver's license, he's twenty-two. He'll be twenty-three in October."

Hawkins did a quick calculation and realized the kid hadn't yet been born the summer Dylan had shown up in Denver. Could be Dylan didn't know any more about the young man in the bed than he did. And at this point, probably knew less.

"You said he'd been shot."

"His left thigh."

Hawkins lifted the sheet. "Skinned at damn close range," he said, dropping the sheet and glancing up at the knife wound again before meeting Loretta's gaze. "Whoever roughed him up was careful not to do any real damage."

"Not careful enough," Loretta said. "We're talking felony assault."

Someone opened the door behind Hawkins, and he turned to see an elegant blonde with a French twist, tight jeans, red heels, and a white T-shirt standing in the doorway with a dark-haired two-year-old boy on her hip. Looking at her, no one would figure her for a world-class operator and first-class sniper, but Hawkins had trained the girl himself, and Skeeter Bang Hart rocked a .308.

"*Holee freaking molee,*" she said, her gaze locking onto

the young man in the bed. "Dylan is going to..."

"Dylan is going to what?" The man in question came up behind Skeeter, and Hawkins figured Liam Magnuson's dance card was complete, and from the look on Dylan's face, not in a good way.

Dylan's stone-cold gaze zeroed in on the bed with unerring accuracy, and after a long, slow look, he turned to his wife. Their gazes met, and in that instant, Hawkins knew Dylan and Skeeter both knew a whole helluva lot more about Liam Dylan Magnuson than he or Loretta did.

CHAPTER FIVE

ON THE NORTHERN OUTSKIRTS OF Denver, Tommy Dunstan stood in the shadows of a fast food joint, eating a hamburger and watching a Rix Towing truck roll up next to Liam's Porsche with a flatbed trailer. Typical.

Wherever the hell Liam had gotten himself off to, Tommy would have bet his left nut the kid would have been back for his car by now – but the damn car was leaving, and the jerk kid was still nowhere in sight.

So, where the hell was he?

Tommy had checked inside the drugstore across the street and the other two fast food joints behind him and come up empty handed. All he had was the car in the burger joint parking lot.

But Big Daddy didn't want the car. Big Daddy wanted the five million dollars his business partner, Momma Margot's first husband, had stolen from him twenty-three years ago. That guy, Liam Dylan Magnuson II, had run off to Geneva, Switzerland with the money, and then up and died with no one but his oldest son there to witness what had happened to the five million.

And that kid, damn Liam Dylan Magnuson number three, had been no fool, even at fifteen years old.

Well, Big Daddy Jack was no fool either. He knew what had happened. With the old Liam dead, Daddy Jack's five million dollars had been stolen by that fancy-shmancy, know-it-all son-of-a-bitch kid who'd disappeared. That's what Big Daddy had always said, that the kid had taken the money and run like a goddamn thief, abandoning his poor Momma Margot and leaving his poor dead daddy lying alone on a cold slab in a Geneva morgue.

Big Daddy said the kid had always been too damn slick for his own good, and too damn slick for anybody else's. No matter how many times Big Daddy had searched for Momma Margot's first son, no matter how many people Big Daddy had sicced on that damn kid, and no matter how much money he'd thrown at the problem, he'd come up empty handed every damn time, no kid, no money – until four days ago when a letter had arrived from a couple of big city, New York lawyers talking about an inheritance for Liam Dylan Magnuson.

Well, hell, to this day, the only Liam Dylan Magnuson anyone could find on the face of the earth was the pansy-assed guitar player. And if the inheritance those lawyers were talking about was the same damn money that had been stolen from Big Daddy, and that money had been sitting in New York all these years, well, hell, the pansy-ass probably thought if he could get there first, he could get away with the millions and keep them for himself – which, Tommy admitted, in no way explained why the pansy-ass had headed west out of Chicago instead of east to New York.

Screw it. Everything to do with that damn money had always been in a twist. Tommy took another bite of his sandwich. *Damn New York City lawyers. Liam's inheritance, my ass.*

That was his own damned inheritance – after Big Daddy passed, of course - and he was closer to getting it than he'd ever been.

Across the street, a police car cruised into the drugstore lot where Tommy had parked his Corvette, and he instinctively stepped back, deeper into the shadows of the burger restaurant. The cop slowed to a crawl when he drove by the Crystal Red Stingray C7, and Tommy secretly flipped him off, the prick.

"Look all you want, asshole." No dumb cop was ever going to own anything as hot as Tommy's red Corvette or for that matter, Liam's 718 Cayman GTS. It was the only thing he and the jerk kid had in common, a love of hot cars.

They could have been friends, or at least halfway decent stepbrothers. But little ole Liam, hell, he'd been a momma's boy from the get-go, spending all his time inside playing the piano or a guitar, and caterwauling. *God,* how that kid could caterwauler. It had been pathetic, especially when all that time, he could have been out in the north Georgia woods where Tommy and his friends had kicked up trouble every day of the week and twice on Sunday.

Sometimes they'd kicked up more trouble than was good for them – but that was all behind Tommy now. Daddy Jack had made sure of it. Tommy had a clean slate, or at least clean enough to have kept him out of prison.

But ole Liam – his slate was a fine mess. He'd done worse than the law-breaking Tommy had done. He'd broken Daddy Jack's rules and Daddy Jack's trust, trying to steal his money. Rock and roll star, Tommy's ass. Metallica, those guys were rock and roll stars, not Liam Jerk-off Magnuson.

"Come on, come on," he muttered, watching the cop. "Move on out of there." He didn't like cops, and he really didn't like them hanging around his car, and he could A-1 guarantee they didn't like him. Back in his younger days, he'd had the rap sheet to prove it.

Tommy's phone vibrated just as another cop cruiser turned into the burger joint's lot.

He checked the caller's name and grimaced. Next to

all these cops, this was the last thing he needed, but he didn't dare not answer.

Swearing to himself, he slid his thumb over the phone's screen and took the call.

"Hey, Daddy."

"Where in the hell are you, boy? Have you found Liam yet?"

Hell, he'd spent half his life answering that one damn question.

"I'm in Colorado, in Denver. Don't have the kid yet, but I'm staring straight at his car." Nothing good ever came from trying to sugarcoat anything for Big Daddy, but that didn't keep Tommy from trying.

"And he's not in it?"

"Uh...no, sir."

Nothing but silence met his admission, and in frustration, Tommy balled up the rest of his sandwich and tossed it in the trash. Dammit. This was where things always went bad between him and Big Daddy.

"So how long have you been staring at his car, boy?"

Goddammit.

"'Bout an hour."

"Put Nate on the phone."

"Can't. Nate ain't here."

"Why not?"

"Well, I've been chasing that sorry-assed kid all night, and Nate and the boys just got a little behind in the Escalade. They'll be here real soon, and we'll nab ole Liam and get his butt back home. Ok?" Easy peasy. Couldn't be simpler.

Except now both cops had pulled up to the flatbed trailer and were walking over to the tow truck driver. Then things really went south.

One of the cops pulled a key out of his pocket.

A damn Porsche key.

And wasn't that just so awful interesting. If the cops

had Liam's Porsche key, then chances were the cops had Liam. Now what in the hell kind of trouble could the kid have gotten himself into out here in the Denver boondocks? He'd hardly been able to stand up after Nate had hit him a couple of times. Not to mention the blood coming off that little knife stripe Tommy had given him, and then there'd been the gunshot scrape on his leg. That sure as hell had gotten the kid's attention.

Tommy grinned.

"Dammit, boy, you listening to me?" Big Daddy's voice broke into Tommy's reverie. "Or are you thinking? You know thinking isn't good for you, boy. You listening to me?'"

No. Tommy wasn't listening. The cop opened the car door and stuck his head inside the Porsche, then jerked it out real fast. He turned aside and coughed a few times, like something smelled real bad in the car, like maybe something or someone had died in there.

Tommy's blood ran cold.

Bobby Lee had only shot the kid across the leg, barely scraped him with the bullet. Nobody died of a scrape, not even a pansy-assed singer in a rock and roll band.

"No, Daddy, I...uh, got to...hell, I'm busy here." He hung up and punched in Nate's number, letting Big Daddy's immediate callback go to voice mail. So help him God, if that dumb kid had gone and died on him, Tommy was going to kill him.

"What?" Nate answered.

"We got us a situation here, a bad situation. You got to...you - " He narrowed his gaze, trying to see inside the Porsche parked on the other side of the lot. Liam had a two-tone leather interior, and the light gray part of the driver's seat was all smeared with something kind of reddish black, quite a bit of it. The seat was a mess.

A bloody mess.

"Nate, boy, you listen to me now. You listen to me

hard. You gotta call that cop buddy of yours in Atlanta. Tell him to call the Denver police and check if the kid got arrested. And the morgue, he better call the morgue, in case...just in case Liam ended up dead."

"Dead? No frickin' way," Nate said. "I only tapped the kid. Tapped him two, maybe three times is all."

"I don't know, Nate. All you did was tap that guy over in Sugar Valley last year, and he still ain't right. But you gotta call that cop in Atlanta, and you tell Bobby Lee to start calling all the hospitals around here. If that boy is still breathing, we gotta find him right now, and I mean *right now*."

Or there was going to be hell to pay, a ball-busting, rat-nasty hell named Big Daddy Jack.

CHAPTER SIX

———

DYLAN SLID HIS GAZE FROM his wife back to the young guy in the bed and felt the knot in his stomach grow even tighter. There were damn few explanations for what he was seeing, and only one made sense. After all these years, after all he'd done and all he'd become, Margot, the faithless bitch known as his mother, had gut-kicked him again. The kid in the bed was undeniable, Dylan's day of reckoning in the flesh.

Looking at him was like looking through a time machine. The arch of his eyebrows, his nose, chin, the shape of his mouth, even the pattern of beard stubble on his jaw, it was all so damned familiar and so damned disconcerting. Dylan saw the same face every morning when he looked in the mirror, only fifteen years older.

Unbelievable.

He glanced at Hawkins and saw one, single, crystal clear question in his teammate's eyes — *"What the fuck? Over."*

Yeah, that was the one, the same overwhelming question frying Dylan's brain.

"No. I don't know him," he said. "But there aren't a lot of options here." He turned to Loretta. "Where'd you get the name Liam Dylan Magnuson? From him?"

That's where this all started, in the exact same place where it had ended twenty-three years ago — with the name. He'd buried that name twice. Once for his father, Liam Dylan Magnuson II, the night he'd died in Geneva, Switzerland, and once for himself, Liam Dylan Magnuson III, two weeks later when he'd become Dylan Hart – and now here it was, after all these years, staring him in the face with his own face, a couple of tattoos, and a gold-hooped earring.

"No," the lieutenant said. "From his driver's license." She nodded at Weisman, and the officer handed Dylan the guy's wallet.

Dylan flipped it open and took another blow. The team's address was handwritten across the back of a business card in the top slot – *Uptown Autos, 738 Steele Street, Denver*. He took the card out, turned it over, and glanced back up at Hawkins.

"Who do we know at the Calhoun Auto Auction in Florida?"

"George Peterson."

"And what does he know about us?"

"Nothing. We're auto dealers, classic stock, high-end cars, and we buy more than we sell. He's the one who showed us that 1967 Ford GT500 EXP a year ago."

Dylan swore under his breath. It wasn't the first time a car had gotten him in trouble – not by a long shot. He put the business card back in the wallet, noted the thick stack of cash still inside, then did a quick calculation off the young guy's driver's license.

After a moment, he took a breath and handed the wallet to Skeeter.

"Check the birthday."

His wife made the same lightning-quick calculation, and a soft flush of color rose in her cheeks.

"Your mother was two months pregnant when your dad died in Geneva."

Two months pregnant, and she'd married Jack Dunstan, his father's business partner, less than four weeks later.

Four of the worst weeks of Dylan's life.

Suddenly, he needed some air.

"What's Liam's status?" Skeeter asked.

"He's a little roughed up," Hawkins said. "Nothing broken, the rest has been stitched, the knife cut on his arm and the gunshot wound across his thigh. He finishes that bag of saline, sleeps off the pain killer, maybe gets a shot of B-12, and he'll be good to take home."

"Gunshot?" Skeeter asked.

"Yeah," Hawkins said. "Whoever got a hold of him was definitely fucking with him."

"Dylan?" Skeeter turned to him. "Dylan," she spoke a little louder, "Superman's right. We need to get Liam out of here."

Of course, Superman was right. But Dylan was stuck on his mother being pregnant and him suddenly having a little brother – after all these years, a brother. No way did the boy in the bed have so much as a chromosome of Jack Dunstan in him.

No, the kid in the bed with the long hair and the gold hoop earring was definitely his blood.

He felt his wife move in closer. "Liam needs to be at Steele Street, Dylan."

Sure. He understood, but...

"Whatever Liam Dylan Magnuson's problem is," Hawkins said, "the Calhoun Auto Auction card says it's got something, maybe everything, to do with you, and given the shape he's in, I think we're the ones to take care of it, to end it."

End it. Right.

But Dylan had already ended all of it years ago. He'd walked away from everyone and everything he'd ever known. He'd buried his past under a mountain of heartache and rage and convinced himself the pain had been conquered.

He'd been wrong.

The proof was lying in the bed, beaten to hell and back, and then someone had tortured him, cut him and tortured him – for what?

Dylan lived with violence, was a skilled practitioner of the violent arts – but that was warfare, combat. This kid was a civilian in a non-war zone, in the heart of the U.S.A. If someone had wanted him dead, he'd be dead. But the injuries weren't fatal and they'd left all his cash alone.

Dylan knew a lot of bastards capable of casual, degrading violence. But he'd only been personally involved with one of those bastards, "Big Daddy" Jack Dunstan. Even thinking about the man made his gut churn, and that he reacted at all royally pissed him off. Jack Dunstan had been long behind him. Long gone from his life.

Until today, over two damn decades later.

Jack had shown up in Geneva within a day of his dad's death. He'd wanted the money, the damn five million he'd accused his father of stealing, and Dylan had figured out very quickly that he would stop at nothing to get it. Absolutely nothing.

Now the worst of that awful time had come home to roost, all his memories looking exactly like what he was seeing – cruel brutality and physical violence. *Déjà-fucking-vu*.

Hawkins was right. The kid being here was about him – and the only things the two of them had in common were a name, a faithless mother, and the bastard she'd married.

He remembered what it had been like to be tracked by Dunstan and his crew of "business associates." Jack Dunstan had wanted him dead, and his mother…his mother hadn't cared enough to rein the bastard in. Or, as he'd sometimes told himself in those early years, she hadn't realized what a scumbag Dunstan truly was.

He'd gotten out of Switzerland and out of Europe by the skin of his teeth – which was more than this kid had managed.

Superman was right. No matter what in the hell was going on, or who was involved, there was only one place Liam Dylan Magnuson belonged tonight – in the SDF fortress at 738 Steele Street.

"Loretta?" he asked the lieutenant.

"Make it so." Loretta nodded.

CHAPTER SEVEN

—◆—

A SMOOTH OPERATING MACHINE, THAT'S WHAT Tommy had created. Between Nate and Bobby Lee, they'd tracked ole Liam down to Denver General Hospital, Room 320. All they had to do was go in and get him. Easy peasy.

Tommy parked in the hospital lot, then got out of the car, sliding out from behind the steering wheel of his Corvette. Leaning back against the door panel, he lit up a cigarette. Nate and Bobby Lee were half an hour behind him, closing in on Denver. Tommy figured the three of them could just pick the boy up and carry him out if Liam couldn't walk on his own. And he wasn't taking any guff from the nurses. Oh hell no. Tommy was the kid's legal stepbrother, come to take him home to Georgia. Any problems, and he'd sic Big Daddy on them.

Life was good. He practically had Liam in his pocket. His phone had stopped ringing – *thank, Gawd*. And his boys were on their way.

He took a long drag off the cigarette and glanced up toward the main entrance of the hospital – and his brain stopped. Just flat-out stopped. The cigarette fell out of his fingers and hit the pavement, and all Tommy could do was stand there and stare at the people coming out of the main door.

He couldn't speak. He couldn't think. But he could

see, and what he saw blew his mind.

Liam Dylan Magnuson – the first one, the slick one who'd stolen Big Daddy's money. The five million lost, but out there, somewhere, unless the damn kid had spent it all.

From the looks of it, he might have spent it on the woman. She was oh-so-fine, unlike anyone Tommy had ever seen, except in a magazine, in the centerfold. Tight jeans, long legs, high heels, blonde hair piled high – good Gawd almighty. She was frickin' hot, even with a kid on her hip.

But the prize, the prize was the man. He and Liam could have been twins, 'cept this guy was older, and Tommy had found him. All those years of clairvoyants, private investigators, and high-end contractors with their tag teams of mercenary hunters had all failed, one-hundred percent.

But not Tommy. His life had just taken a hard right into "You Owe Me, Daddy Jack," big time, for-fucking-ever.

The threesome coming out of the hospital were headed toward a 1969 Camaro Z28, blue metallic, a real classic – and Tommy had to wonder if hot cars ran in the blood. While they buckled the kid into a car seat, Tommy slid back in behind the wheel of his Corvette and got on the horn to Nate.

He and Bobby Lee could handle Liam. Tommy was going after the big fish. Ten percent, that's the deal he was cutting with Big Daddy. If his father wanted the real deal, it was going to cost him.

Dumb Dunstan – that had been his nickname in school. But no more. He had the score of the decade.

He fired up the 'Vette, then stopped to take a breath while he waited for Nate to answer. He was so excited, he was shaking.

"Settle down, boy, just settle down," he whispered to

himself. "And don't screw this up."

Alright. Okay. He was fine. "Just ease on out there, boy, and follow that bastard home."

"What bastard?" Nate asked, picking up the call on the other end.

"Nothing," Tommy said. "Just nothing. I got something I gotta do. So, you and Bobby Lee get here and get Liam out of this damn hospital. Hole up somewhere, and I'll call you when I'm done. And no more tapping him, or shooting him. We're done with all that, you hear?"

"Sure, I hear you. But you better tell me what it is you think you've gotta do, Tommy, because whatever it is, Daddy Jack gave you a job, and he expects you to do it, not go gallivanting around Denver."

"I ain't gallivanting, Nate. You just get here and get Liam." He hung up and tossed the phone into the passenger seat – then followed the Camaro out of the hospital parking lot.

---

*Screw you...*the words died on Nate's lips. This was stupid. He wasn't busting into a hospital and getting Liam without Tommy. That was crazy. He wasn't related to the kid. So how in the hell was he supposed to pull off this stupid plan? Just go in there and kidnap him?

Oh, hell no. He could see that going south in a heartbeat. Tommy was too damn dumb to breathe, let alone give orders, and Nate would be damned if he –

His phone rang, and one look had him swearing under his breath. His luck couldn't be this damn bad.

The phone rang again, and he sank lower in the driver's seat of the Escalade. He didn't want to answer.

But he had to answer.

Looking out the passenger window, he gave Bobby Lee a "get-in-here-right-now-you-dumbass" wave of his hand. Bobby Lee was worse than a kid, slurping down sodas and needing to pee every hundred miles. Pathetic.

The phone rang again, and he knew there'd be hell to pay if he let it go to voicemail.

Bracing himself, he answered, "Yeah," and a big ole wall of Daddy Jack Dunstan tore into him like a combine.

By the time it was all over, he'd told Daddy Jack everything he could think of and then some.

"Wassup?" Bobby Lee asked when he got in the car. "Who you talkin' to?"

"Daddy Jack," Nate said, giving the kid a long look. "I told him you shot Liam and put him in the hospital, and he ain't none too happy about it. He is on his way, Bobby Lee. Getting on a plane to Denver."

It was just a few words, but Bobby Lee's face went whiter with every one.

"Now we got to get to that damn hospital and get that boy out of there before Daddy Jack gets here, or there is gonna be hell to pay, and you, boy, are gonna be the one writing the check."

Bobby Lee started to shake, and Nate stepped on the gas.

CHAPTER EIGHT

———

TWO BLOCKS FROM THE HOSPITAL, Skeeter took another glance in the Camaro's side view mirror.

"Who do you know with a Crystal Red Stingray C7?"

"Only the guy who was hanging out in the hospital parking lot," Dylan said. "The tubby backwoods boy with the curly blond hair wearing a green and black plaid shirt and a pair of shit-kickers that look like he might actually spend time kicking shit."

"Yeah," Skeeter agreed. "That's the only one I know, too." She paused for a moment before adding, "He's got Georgia plates."

"I noticed," Dylan said. He'd been born and raised in Georgia, and he'd bet the bank his mother and Jack Dunstan still lived there. If Grady hadn't been in the car, he'd have slammed on the brakes, and he and Skeeter could have figured out the tubby backwoods boy damn quick. Instead, he was going with Plan B. "If he follows us home, we'll shake him down there. If not, we'll get Loretta to run his plates."

"Agreed," Skeeter said. "You do the shaking. I'll take Grady upstairs and get Creed down on the street to do the welcoming honors."

"That'll put the fear of God in the backwoods boy."

"Hell, yeah," she said, slipping her phone out of the back pocket of her jeans.

SDF's Jungle Boy had a war face guaranteed to strike

fear in the hearts of lesser men and deadly respect in the hearts of his equals. But so did all the guys at SDF, and, admittedly, so did she and Red Dog.

"It's been a helluva morning," she said, punching up Creed's phone number.

"Harrowing," he agreed.

"What are we going to do about it, Dylan? How far are we going to take this?"

"I'm not going to kill him, if that's what you're asking," he said, and she knew he was talking about Jack Dunstan, not the backwoods boy in the 'Vette. "But, if Dunstan is involved in this, I'm going to destroy him. I left him alone all these years, because I didn't want to think about him. But I'm thinking about him now. A smart guy would never have let that happen."

CHAPTER NINE

*T*HIS JUST AIN'T RIGHT, NATE thought, getting into the hospital elevator on the main floor with Bobby Lee. But dammit, he didn't have a choice. Daddy Jack had made that clear.

"That damn Tommy should be here," he said. "We aren't any kin to Liam. If anything goes wrong, we haven't got a leg to stand on."

"I'm Liam's kin," Bobby Lee said. "Second cousin twice-removed on my momma's side."

"Whatever the hell that means," Nate muttered, hitting the button for the third floor. "Twice-removed, my ass. Here," he took his comb out of his pocket and handed it to Bobby Lee. "Clean yourself up."

Like that was even possible. Bobby Lee Raynor, a.k.a. Ratface Raynor was pure scrawny from his old boots to his greasy black hair. And Nate didn't care what the boy said, Bobby Lee came by his nickname honestly. The kid was twenty years old and looked like a Georgia roof rat.

Nate tucked in his polo shirt, hiding a small blood smear, and "gig-lined" his belt buckle. *One hundred percent shipshape,* he assured himself - *and yet, somehow, headed straight into the crapper with Bobby Lee.*

God, he'd thought he was smarter than this.

He caught his reflection in the elevator's chrome control panel and flexed his arms. Even with the reflection a bit woozy and distorted, he could see his muscles bulge and strain against the tight sleeves of his polo shirt – and he felt his mood lift a little.

Oh, yeah, some guys just had a knack for looking good – he glanced over at Bobby Lee - *and some guys just didn't.*

"Straighten up your shirt, Bobby Lee. I can see your pea-shooter sticking out of your shoulder rig." As if anybody carried a damn 1911 wannabe chambered for .22 in a shoulder holster. Bobby Lee rearranged the collared shirt he was wearing over his T-shirt, pulling the front two sides closer together to cover the holster.

Damn kid, shooting Liam on the leg. Tommy and Bobby Lee both needed their heads examined to see if they had any brains in them at all. How Big Jack Dunstan had fathered an idiot like Tommy was beyond Nate's comprehension.

On the third floor, he shoved Bobby Lee out ahead of him, then checked the signs for directions, and turned left. They played it cool, just a couple of guys visiting a sick friend.

When they breezed past the nurse's station, Nate's confidence rose. Easy in, easy out.

At Room 320, he looked through the narrow window in the door and saw Liam lying in the bed. The kid was asleep and had some tubes stuck in him. Nate figured they could handle the tubes. But if Liam was out cold, it was going to look damn funny to have him and Bobby Lee carrying the kid out.

It had been a crappy plan from the get go. Par for the course when the guy coming up with the plan was Tommy Dunstan. Dumb Dunstan, they'd called him in school.

Still looking through the window, Nate devised his own plan.

A knife, he decided, pulling his folding knife out of his pocket and thumbing it open. Whatever medical equipment might be attached to Liam needed to be done away with quickly and efficiently. The only way to do it was to get in fast, cut the boy loose, and hustle him to the elevator.

"Come on," he said to Bobby Lee, and they pushed through the door of Room 320 like they belonged there.

They did not.

Two cops they had not seen through the narrow window turned and leveled identical "cop stares" at them, giving Nate a moment's pause – which turned out to be a moment too long. Inside of a second, he'd been grabbed and slammed up against the wall so hard he saw stars. His knife clattered to the floor, his left arm was trapped, and his right arm was pulled up hard behind his back by someone else he had not seen through the window. He heard Bobby Lee make a dash for it, and saw one of the cops tackle him, and then another damned awful thing happened. Bobby Lee's pistol came out of his shoulder rig and skittered across the tile floor – in front of a pair of cops and whoever was about to break his arm. Nate struggled to free himself, but the more he struggled, the more pain the guy administered.

Geezus. The guy was mother-freakin' strong.

"Well, I gotta say, this just makes my day," Lieutenant Loretta said, walking over to where Hawkins had one of Liam's "visitors" hauled up against the wall. "It is just so much easier when the bad guys come to us, rather than making us chase them all over hell and gone."

She snapped a pair of handcuffs on the man and stepped back. "What's your name, son?"

All she got was a narrowed, brown-eyed glare from an over-juiced gym rat who looked like he worked out twenty-four hours a day and yet had already proven he wasn't tough enough. Despite being dressed in a nice pair of black slacks and a pale blue polo shirt, he looked like bad news and trouble all rolled into one – an opinion reinforced by what appeared to be a bloodstain on the lower hem of his shirt, as if he might have wiped his hand there after he'd hit somebody a few times. His knuckles, indeed, looked like he'd been hitting somebody or something pretty damn hard.

She picked up the knife and closed it.

And then there was the gun.

"Do you have a concealed carry permit for your pistol?" she asked the guy on the floor, bending down to pick up the gun.

"Don't need no permit. I'm from Georgia."

Cripes, she thought. Could it really be this easy?

"What do you think, Superman?"

"I think these two belong to you, *Jefe*"

"Agreed. Weisman, call this in and get a couple of officers over here to pick up the trash...uh, excuse me, to *escort* these two fine gentlemen to our precinct. And read them their rights."

Weisman finished handcuffing the smaller man on the floor, then hauled him to his feet and walked him over to face the wall, next to his buddy. "Get on your knees and stay down. *You have the right to remain silent...*"

"On your knees," Hawkins said to the guy he was holding, helping him out by pushing him down. "Stay put."

"Superman my ass," the guy said under his breath, kneeling nose-to-the-wall next to his buddy. The position was awkward enough to make a fast getaway next to impossible. "I could take you in a fair fight."

"Maybe, *chingaleto*," Hawkins conceded to the big guy, "but I never fight fair."

"There may be more from where these two came

from," Loretta said. "I'd appreciate it if you'd stay until after they're hauled downtown."

"I'm not going anywhere without my new best friend, Lieutenant." He gestured toward the bed. "You can count on it."

CHAPTER TEN

TOMMY PULLED UP TO THE curb on Steele Street and parked on the opposite side of the street from the blue Camaro. He was good, so good. He'd tailed them all the way from the hospital, a couple of miles back, into the heart of downtown Denver and had them in his sights.

The woman got out of the car, got the kid, and headed into an old building, while the prize of the century stayed put in the driver's seat.

Tommy checked the numbered address on the building, 738, then took a picture of the numbers, carefully fitting the street sign in the foreground. Satisfied with the photo, he added a text message – *I found him, the asshole who stole your five million. He ain't dead. Not yet, anyway* ☺

He hit SEND, and grinned. That ought to fry Big Daddy's balls real good...and get the old bastard on the next plane to Denver.

His grin faded. That was the last thing he needed. Dammit, he should have thought things through a little better, kept the news to himself awhile longer.

His phone dinged, and Tommy swore. But he didn't dare ignore the incoming text.

Dammit, boy, Big Daddy had replied. *You listen to me, and you listen real good. Don't do anything. Stay fucking put. I'm on my way, and we'll blow this bastard right out of his rat hole.*

No way, Tommy thought. He wasn't waiting for anybody. This was his game to run, and it was simple. All he had to do was stroll over to the other side of the street and get the "old" Liam. Just walk up on him with his gun drawn and kidnap the bastard, get him in the 'Vette and take off with him. Hell, take off with him all the way to Georgia, and Big Daddy could eat his dust.

Piece of cake.

Right.

"Hey, buddy, you got a cigarette?" A voice came out of nowhere.

Geezus! Tommy 'bout jumped out of his pants. *Geezus.*

A damn long-haired hippy leaned in the 'Vette's driver's side window.

"Get off my damn car." He scowled and gave the street a glance, wondering where in the hell the guy had come from.

"Sure, man," the guy said, but didn't back off an inch. "You got a cigarette?"

Tommy gave him a quick once-over and realized "hippy" probably wasn't the right word, despite the guy's long blonde hair, not unless he was the world's cleanest and most damned fittest hippy.

"Yeah," he said, reaching in his shirt pocket. "Yeah, I got a cigarette." Hell, he pulled out the whole pack and shoved it at the guy. "Now get outta here."

"Sure, man." The "hippy" took the cigarettes. "But I was wondering if you had a gun."

Startled by the question, it took Tommy a moment to give the guy a "you must be the world's biggest idiot" look. It was nobody's business but his own that he had a snub-nosed .38 in the Corvette's glove box.

"And my buddy over there" the guy gestured to the other side of the Corvette – "wonders why you followed him from the hospital."

Tommy jerked his head to the right and froze solid from his brains to his balls. The only thing moving was his heart, and it was red-lined.

The big bore of a .45 was leveled at his head, held steady in a strong hand, and above the bore was a face he knew all too damn well, but older, and crueler – and if there was one thing Tommy knew about, it was cruelty. Big Daddy had been a fine teacher about cruelty.

"You carrying?" the "old" Liam Dylan Magnuson asked. "Or do you keep a gun in the glove box?"

It took an eternity for Tommy to process the question, but it finally cut its way through the deep fog of fear muddling him up. Not that cutting through the fog did much good.

"B-b-b...b-b...b-b-b..." Tommy couldn't tear his gaze away from the man leaning in the 'Vette's passenger side window, and so help him God, he could not stop blubbering – even though he was damn sure his life depended on it.

"Okay, I got it," the old Liam said, reaching in and popping the glove box open. "Give my friend your wallet."

"Wa...wa-wa...wa-wa-wa..." Tommy watched as the old Liam cleared the .38 before dropping it into his pocket. But Tommy still had his knife, thank God.

"Yeah, your wallet," old Liam reminded him, and gave the .45 a little lift.

Tommy felt a dribble of pee soak his pants. *Geezus!* Oh, sweet Jesus, he could die here, right in gawddamn Denver and no-one would ever know what had happened to him.

For cripes sake, grab hold of yourself, boy, he told himself. *Grab the hell hold of yourself.*

With effort, he steadied himself enough to start fumbling around, doing his damnedest to obey.

Pulling his shirt up a bit, he finally got the wallet out

of his back pocket and handed it over to the "hippy."

"He's got a knife, Jungle Boy," the old Liam said. "Sheathed on his belt. And get his phone."

Jungle Boy? And how had old Liam guessed about his damn knife?

Tommy looked down where he'd pulled his shirt up. Oh, no guess required – the sheath was exposed for all the world to see, with his knife sticking out of it.

"Hand it over, pardner," Jungle Boy said. And yes, Tommy could see some Tarzan in the guy, more than he could see any hippy. "All of it. Keep the knife sheathed."

Tommy finally got the knife sheath off his belt, wishing to hell he hadn't peed himself and praying to God he didn't do it again.

The long-haired guy took his knife and his phone, then flipped the wallet open. "You know anyone named Thomas Edward Dunstan?" he asked the "old" Liam.

"Tommy Dunstan," the man said, his gaze fixing on Tommy and growing even colder. "Guaranteed, son, this is not going to be one of your better days. Get out of the car."

CHAPTER ELEVEN

—◆—

MAN, OH, MAN, SKEETER THOUGHT, watching Liam from where she sat at the head of her and Dylan's kitchen table. Hawkins, Liam's self-appointed bodyguard, was at the other end of the table. Gillian and Travis, Dylan's mandated, high-end additions to Liam's Personal Security Detail, PSD, were sitting across from the young man, looking like they could kick every ass on the block - because they could. Dinner was leftovers from yesterday's 4th of July celebration, and almost everyone was talking about cars — muscle cars, sports cars, clunkers they'd owned, and the fastest they'd raced.

No one was going anywhere near the five-hundred-pound gorilla in the room — the who, what, when, where, and why of Liam Dylan Magnuson being at Steele Street. He was Dylan's mystery to unravel, and they were all waiting for Dylan to show up — which apparently was going to happen about the same time hell froze over.

Skeeter had to work at not calling her husband and telling him to get his butt out of the basement. She needed a little help here, almost as much as his little brother — his extremely sexy-hot little brother, so help her God.

"And we've got a 1969 Yenko 427 Nova down in the garage," Hawkins said, reaching for another slice of watermelon.

Liam looked up from his mostly untouched plate. "A Yenko 427 Nova?" A note of awe edged the young guy's voice, and Skeeter felt a little relief. Finally, something had caught his attention besides the front door.

Sure, she understood. Only one thing had brought him to Denver – Dylan. But even two hours after Liam and Hawkins had arrived home from the hospital, Dylan was still with Creed and the poor sap Tommy Dunstan, who was undoubtedly having one of the worst nights of his life.

But that was Tommy Dunstan's problem.

Her problem was Liam Dylan Magnuson the Fourth, not the Third. She knew the "Third" inside and out. But Liam the "Fourth," or Liam Magnus, as he preferred to be called, well, he was something else. He looked rode hard, put away wet, and like he'd run through a gauntlet – and every time she looked at him, which was way too often, she was struggling a little with her heart.

"Yeah, the Nova," Travis added. "She's a sublime bitch, and you are gonna flat-out fall in love with her."

"Bitch?" Gillian let out a short laugh. "The Nova's a sweetheart, Liam, which is why Skeeter named her Mercy."

"Mercy?" Liam shifted his gaze to Skeeter, and her heart damn near sank into her stomach. The resemblance between him and Dylan was mind-blowing.

"I, uh, used to race her at the Midnight Doubles," she said. "And the Nova never showed any mercy. She took every race she ran."

"Cool," he said.

Yeah, cool, she thought. *But not as cool as you, rock and roll boy.*

Besides his arm and leg, the doctors had put a couple of stitches in the side of his face, up along his cheekbone. He was going to have another scar, but with his looks – the whole silky-haired, hard-bodied, "I should be an underwear model for Calvin –

"Skeet, can you pass the potato salad?" Hawkins interrupted her train of thought.

"Uh, sure," she said, dragging her gaze and her attention back to the table and the, uh, potato salad.

She handed it off to Travis, and her gaze automatically drifted back to Liam.

Rock and roll star, indeed. He was disturbingly sexy, even all beat up. And her husband had looked exactly like him at that age, devastatingly gorgeous, except without the tattoos, the long hair, and the gold hoop earring. Girls must have been throwing themselves and their underwear and God only knew what else at him every damn day of his life at twenty-two – and she'd have been eleven years old. He wouldn't have noticed her no matter what she'd thrown at him.

Why that should be twisting her up was not beyond her comprehension. It was embarrassingly simple. Jealousy.

She was jealous of all the girls who'd fallen crazy in love with her husband before she'd been old enough to even be in the game.

And now here he was, sitting right in front of her, like he'd materialized out of a time-machine – Dylan at twenty-two years old, but not really Dylan, just close enough to scramble her brain.

"So, Skeet," Gillian said, "have you heard anything from Kid and Nikki? When are they getting home?"

Skeeter looked over at her friend, a little confused. "Uh, they're still in Paris. You know how they love Paris." Everybody at Steele Street knew how much Kid Chaos, an SDF sniper, and his artist wife, Nikki, loved Paris. And everyone knew they'd be home next week.

But if Gillian's expression was any clue, that hadn't been the point of her question. The real question was "Do you know you're staring a hole in that boy?"

Yes, she knew. Thank you.

Skeeter deliberately ran her gaze over Gillian and across Travis, operators professionally known as Red Dog and Angel, and her unspoken question – when she returned her attention to Gillian - was equally clear, as in "What "edge of the world" are the two of you dropping off tonight?"

They were geared up, gunned up, and had left their rucksacks by the door. Dinner with the Steele Street crew and Dylan's *doppelgänger*, she was certain, had not been on their agenda tonight.

They were mission-ready, but not for a Steele Street mission.

Most of their work had gotten so black and came from so far up the food chain at the Department of Defense, she didn't have a clue what the two of them were doing out there in the big, bad world anymore. Neither did General Grant, which had surprised the hell out of her.

But if the tubby backwoods boy, Tommy Dunstan, and the two hicks Lieutenant Loretta had booked, were any indication, working a PSD for Liam Magnus was way below their pay grade. And yet, Dylan had ordered Gillian and Travis to the thirteenth floor – which made her wonder what kind of intel Dylan had gotten out of Tommy Dunstan, and what the stakes really were in this fiasco.

As if on cue, Travis's phone rang. He answered with a single word, "Go."

A second later, he hung up, nodded at Gillian, and as one, they rose from the table.

"Good luck," Gillian said, leaning over the table to shake Liam's hand.

"Gents." Travis followed suit, shaking Liam's hand and giving Hawkins a nod before turning to Skeeter. "Skeet, thanks for dinner."

Without another word or wasted movement, they

crossed the room, hoisted their rucksacks to their shoulders, and walked out the door.

Gone. Just like that.

But still on her radar. Something more than just the endless, black-on-black mystery missions was happening with the two of them. She had a few ideas, some of which made sense, and one that was downright unthinkable – but she was thinking it.

Maybe it was time for her to hack into Dr. Brandt's files at Walter Reed Medical Center and find out what the hell was really going on with Red Dog and the Angel Boy.

Well, now that The Avengers *have left,* Liam thought, watching the door close. *Damn.*

He'd seen a lot of things in his life, but he'd never seen anything like the two people who'd walked out the door – ripped, armed to the teeth, beautiful in a real badass sort of way, and serious as a pair of heart attacks.

Hawkins – another certifiable badass - had called the woman "Red Dog." Could a name get any cooler? And Red Dog had called her boyfriend "Angel."

Red Dog and Angel – oh, hell, there was a song in there somewhere.

What a night.

What a freakin' crazy night.

When he'd gone looking for Dylan Hart, he'd expected to find a high-end car dealer. But these guys were no car dealers, no matter how much iron they had in their multi-story garage.

So, what in the hell had he gotten himself into? Some sort of off-the-grid paramilitary group? That was the question that had kept his head down through most of the meal - that and wondering why his brother hadn't shown up yet. Hawkins and Skeeter had told him Dylan was here, in the building. So where in the hell was he hiding out, and why?

Because he doesn't want anything to do with you, punk.

Yeah, yeah, Liam got it, but he hadn't dragged himself halfway across the country to get stiff-armed by some joker who didn't think he was worth the time of day.

Screw Dylan Hart. He hadn't come here looking for a handout. He had the guy's letter from the New York lawyer — and every reason to believe it didn't have a damn thing to do Daddy Jack's "missing" five million dollars. No, Liam would have bet his Porsche and his Stratocaster the money had been sitting in Switzerland for the last twenty-three years.

Whether his brother showed up or not, anything their dad had left with the lawyer belonged to Dylan Hart, not Liam. Their dad hadn't even known another kid was on the way — a fact his mother had impressed upon him many times over the years, trying to convince him he needed to treat Big Jack more like a father, show him some respect.

Not very damn likely, not then, and sure as hell not now.

Cripes. He hated to think he'd gotten the crap beaten out of him for nothing. But he was only giving this party another fifteen minutes, then he was out of here, calling a cab and moving his sorry ass to the Four Seasons Hotel. He didn't have a doubt in his mind that Christian Hawkins could be counted on to deliver the letter and a message.

He glanced down at the pack lying on the floor next to his chair.

Tommy had torn through the backpack in Grand Island, bitching about all the stupid junk stuffed inside, bitching about not finding any money, or a check, and completely missing the envelope in a secret inside pocket, and totally dismissing the real prize – half a dozen old paperback books, their covers worn and dog-eared. Disgusted, Tommy had shoved all the "junk" back into the pack and tossed it into the Porsche.

God, all these years, he'd been holding onto the name, hoping he had a brother who might still be alive, a brother who had out-run and out-foxed Big Daddy Jack Dunstan across the whole of Europe.

Ten more minutes. That was it. Then he was out of here.

He gave the woman sitting at the other end of the table a quick glance. Just as quickly, he looked back at his plate, keeping his head down. Yeah, just ten more minutes of driving himself crazy.

Skeeter Bang Hart. She was tearing him up – so gorgeous he could barely look at her.

And that was a first. Gorgeous women threw themselves at him from one end of the globe to the other.

But not this girl.

She was no groupie. The scar across her forehead spoke of tough times, or a bar fight that hadn't gone her way. She was sleekly muscled, built like a centerfold, and had a folding knife clipped inside her front pocket.

She was also wearing a big diamond ring on her left hand.

Married. To his brother. A sister-in-law – and that, baby, could never work.

He at least had enough brains left to know that.

"Anybody ready for cake?" she asked, and he heard her chair slide away from the table.

He looked up – he couldn't help himself – and watched her cross the full length of the kitchen to the counter, his gaze glued to her ass the whole way. High heels, long legs, sinfully tight jeans - he felt a little like he was dying.

And Hawkins had seen enough. Time to call the boss before somebody blew a fuse.

Dylan answered on the first ring. "*Yo, Cristo.*"

Hawkins was brief and to the point. "Get up here asap and bring a bucket of water."

CHAPTER TWELVE

———

*B*UCKET OF WATER, MY ASS, Dylan thought, coming to a stop when he opened the door into the apartment. Baby brother needed a fire hose turned on him.

Not that Dylan didn't understand the boy's problem. Skeeter was a knock-out. She was also his, but she could hardly keep her eyes off the rock and roll boy any better than the rock and roll boy could keep his eyes off her.

He stood in the doorway for another moment, observing the situation unfolding in the dining room – until he'd seen enough.

Hell. He was too old for this.

The only person completely unfazed, the only person eating their cake, was Hawkins, who, unlike the other two people at the table, had noticed him the instant he'd walked in the door.

With a quick glance at the two "youngsters" at the table, Hawkins gave him a slight shrug and took another bite of cake.

He got the message. He was on his own here.

Hell – and he hated to say it, but he understood Skeeter's reaction. Even beat up, the kid was good-looking, exceptionally, like a high-end model, which he had been a year ago for some Italian designer's "rock stars wear my men's cologne" advertising campaign.

Dylan had Creed to thank for that bit of information,

along with the photos the Jungle Boy had found on the internet of the guitar hero rising from the sea like a tattooed god with the cologne's name circling him in golden, sun-kissed letters.

Honestly, Dylan was damn glad he was none the worse for wear, but the kid had been a helluva lot easier to look at when he'd been asleep in the hospital bed. Finding him sitting at the dining room table made the situation far more real – seismic-shift real. A brother.

"Skeet," he said, giving her a head's up, in case she'd like to help him out by at least trying not to stare at the kid.

Two heads turned toward him, but it was Skeeter's gaze he met first. To his surprise, and odd sense of relief, she looked rattled, not infatuated.

Alright, he thought, even more curious. It took a lot to shake his bad girl.

"Babe," she said, rallying with a small smile. "Plenty of food left, if you're hungry. Is Creed coming up?"

"After he checks on a couple of things."

He shifted his gaze to Liam, who'd taken Dylan's instant of inattention to sit up straighter, to square his shoulders, to ready himself.

Nice try, kid, Dylan thought, but this was no contest, no matter how much Italian cologne the guy had sold.

And yet, looking at the rock and roll wonder face-to-face was enough to set Dylan back a few more degrees. While nobody was ever going to ask him to model anything other than a .45 or a combat knife, the resemblance between him and his brother was uncanny, including the dark-eyed, calculating gaze he was getting in return.

Oh, yeah, he knew that look. There was a definite "throw down" in the younger man's eyes, and behind the challenge, a shade of uncertainty.

Well, little brother, that makes two of us, he thought.

"How are you feeling?" he asked.

"Good," Liam said.

Dylan nodded. "Glad to hear it." And yes, that was him at his nurturing best. And yes, he knew it was pathetic and probably made him some kind of heartless bastard, and he was pretty sure if he asked around, he could get a "Yes, boss," on that point from just about everybody he knew – except Skeeter.

She knew where his heart was.

He ran his gaze over the younger man again, noting the stitches on the left-side of his face, the bruising under his right eye, the long-healed scar along his jaw, and the bandage peeking out from under the sleeve of his T-shirt, where Tommy had cut him with a knife.

That really pissed him off.

And don't even ask him about the gunshot wound on the kid's leg.

He took a breath and moved forward.

Sitting down at the table, he reached into his pocket for his antacids – then stopped. He already felt ancient compared to the guitar hero. No need to go ahead and prove the point.

What he needed was to take control, figure the kid out.

Right.

He needed to set the kid straight and move forward.

Right.

And protect him.

At all costs.

Put a bodyguard on him.

Someone who could take down guys like Tommy Dunstan, Nate Martell, and Bobby Lee Raynor with one arm tied behind his back.

Dylan knew a lot of guys like that, had known most of them since he was sixteen.

Okay, it was settled then. The kid was getting a

bodyguard.

"Dunstan, Martell, and Raynor are all in custody for felony assault and half a dozen other charges," he said. "Chances are they'll all be doing time for what happened last night at the truck stop."

"Well...maybe not all of them." The kid shook his head. "Nate and Bobby Lee, yeah, but Daddy Jack will never let Tommy go to prison. He'll do whatever it takes, pay whatever it takes, to save Tommy."

Dylan didn't get second-guessed very often, if ever, and truthfully, he liked it that way.

"Well, Jack Dunstan's luck has been running out all day" - he checked his watch – "and in another hour or so, it's going to hit rock bottom in a gutter so deep, he'll never dig his way out.He won't be able to save his own ass, let alone Tommy's." Cool, calm, collected, that was him, taking care of business.

The kid shook his head again, tilting it to one side with a very doubtful grin curving his mouth, and Dylan's whole supply of cool and calm went up in flames.

"There's nothing I'd love to see more than that sonuvabitch go down," Liam said, "but he's got two congressmen in his pocket, and he runs them pretty hard."

Dylan had seen that grin before, that tilt of the head, and suddenly he was fifteen again, being his father's righthand man for the Geneva trip. In a dozen ways he hadn't noticed when the kid had been out cold in the hospital bed, Liam looked more like their father than Dylan had at any age. The kid's smile had slammed the news home in a heartbeat.

And man, that hurt like a bitch, in all those dark places Dylan thought he'd put long behind him.

Maybe he needed that antacid after all.

Taking a breath, he took the pathetic roll of antacids out of his pocket and threw a handful into his mouth.

CRAZY HEARTS 61

Then he gave Hawkins a quick glance, tapped the table with two fingers, and said, "Stranahan's."

A cry for help, if he'd ever given one.

Hawkins rose from the table.

Dylan turned his attention back to Liam, knowing something a little stiffer than fifteen-year-old Scotch was on its way, a little liquid courage to help him sort through this unfuckingbelievable situation and the kid's smile.

Hawkins had already filled him in on last night's sequence of events and how it had all come down according to Liam. The whole night had been damn crude and disturbingly violent, and all of it had been corroborated by Tommy Dunstan.

Proving to have the backbone of an invertebrate, the backwoods boy had blubbered all the way from the Corvette to Steele Street's basement, confessing everything he could think of, from last night to his notable rap sheet of misdemeanors, another possible felony or two from a few years back unrelated to Liam, the passcode to his phone, and all about Big Daddy Jack telling him this was the best chance he'd ever had to get the five million dollars stolen from him by Dylan and his "daddy" – a newsflash that had raised Creed's eyebrows damn near to his hairline with a clear look of *What the fuck, kemo sabe?*

Tommy said the inheritance and the law stuff was all laid out in a letter a New York City law firm had sent to Liam, and that Liam had wrestled Tommy's copy of the letter off him in Chicago, then flown the coop.

Wrestled? Dylan had thought, eyeing the backwoods boy. The kid he'd seen in the hospital bed hadn't looked like he could wrestle anything off two-hundred-plus pounds of backwoods mean with a grudge.

But Tommy wasn't worried about losing his copy, he'd said, because Big Daddy had the original, and that's the one they would take to New York to get the money from the lawyers.

"So you and your father think the money is in New York with the lawyers who sent the letter?" Dylan had asked, knowing damn well it wasn't.

"Yes, sir." Tommy had nodded. "It's right in the letter – inheritance. They've got the money."

Well, they've got something, Dylan had thought. *But it sure as hell isn't the money.*

He knew where every dollar of the initial five million had gone over the years. He also knew the portfolio had more than tripled in value, and that a good-sized chunk of it was still in Geneva, Switzerland, securely stashed at Credit Suisse in an investment account. The rest of it was securely invested in the thirteen floors rising above them at 738 Steele Street, a prime piece of Denver real estate gaining in value every month for well over a decade, and now jointly owned by him and Skeeter. He'd put her on the deed within a week of getting married, swearing to her that she would never be without a home.

He'd also put her on the account at Credit Suisse. The work they did was dangerous. If anything happened to him, he didn't want there to be any doubt about who owned the account.

"All we need is little Liam to go with us to see those damn lawyers and get that damn money," Tommy had said.

Not gonna happen, Dylan had thought.

At that point, Creed had held up Tommy's phone, showing him a pair of texts, and Dylan's night had been complete. Jack Dunstan was headed to Denver and had the Steele Street address along with a photo of the building. Perfect.

"And Big Daddy gave me the job of goin' and gettin' Liam," Tommy had said. "And we was to drag his ass back to Georgia any way we could. That's what Big Daddy said – *any way we could.*"

As far as Dylan knew, the "my daddy told me to do it" defense had never kept anybody out of jail, and he could guarantee it hadn't tonight. Officer Weisman had picked up Tommy an hour ago.

Jack Dunstan didn't know it yet, but his world had already started crumbling. His son was sitting in the slammer, and a couple of phone calls Dylan had made earlier in the day had unleashed a rolling tide of inevitable destruction headed in the bastard's direction.

But Liam was still getting a bodyguard. Dylan needed to be able to sleep at night.

A double shot of Stranahan's Colorado Whiskey appeared next to him on the table, along with the rest of the bottle. Hawkins laid a piece of paper next to the bottle, then sat back down to his cake.

Dylan glanced down at the note – *Panama a no-go. V.N. an asset. Langley has their own guy on it.*

Well, that beat all, he thought. Vasily Nikolayevich was working with the CIA. The spooks had done a damn good job of keeping that information to themselves. Dylan was only grateful to have found out before he and Hawkins had landed in Central America.

Thank God for little favors.

He emptied half the glass of whiskey in one swallow before levelling his gaze at his brother.

"So, you ran into George Peterson at the Calhoun Auto Auction." It was a statement, not a question.

"Yeah. The boys and I were down there looking for cars, and then I hear some guy yelling *Hey Dylan... Dylan Hart!* So naturally, I turn around, looking for you, because" – Liam paused, his gaze glancing off Hawkins before returning to Dylan – "because, man, I've been looking for you my whole life."

Dylan didn't budge, not a muscle, just sat there calmly,

listening. But his mind was racing. The kid had been looking for Dylan Hart, for his whole life? How in the hell was that even possible?

"But then the guy gets closer," Liam was saying, "and he's looking straight at me, and I see him realize" - the barest flicker of a grin curved his mouth again – "I see him realize I'm way too young to be Dylan Hart, too young to be Old Man Hart."

Old Man Hart?

Geezus. Dylan almost laughed out loud – but didn't. The kid had balls. He had to give him that. But what he'd said? That didn't make sense. No one from his past had known his name, except, apparently, his little brother – who hadn't even been born the night Liam Dylan Magnuson III had become Dylan Hart. So what the hell?

"Old Man Hart?" he prompted, curious to hear what else the kid had to say.

"Yeah," Liam nodded, his grin widening. "I didn't know exactly how old you'd be, but with Big Jack bitching about you and the money you stole from him every time he got drunk, I eventually put the dates and numbers together enough to figure you must have been about fifteen or so when Dad died in Geneva and you disappeared off the map. I'd sure as hell like to know how you did it. I never got farther than the Florida Keys. But you...man, you fucking disappeared. Must have been amazing."

It was the oddest damn thing, Dylan thought. The people sitting at the table knew him better than anyone else on the planet. Then along comes a total stranger, a family member who he hadn't even known existed, and his entire life's secrets come spilling out like water out of a breached dam.

He looked over at Hawkins, whose steady, unflinching gaze was sending a very clear message – *We need to talk, boss.*

Yeah, Dylan had some explaining to do, except to Skeeter. She knew everything – the money, his father, his mother, Geneva, Jack Dunstan. She knew everything except how rough and deadly the situation in Geneva had actually been. But his crew didn't know any of it. Hell, Tommy Dunstan was at best a step-family member, and he'd shocked the bejeezies out of Creed with his "you and your dad stole five million dollars" accusation down in the basement.

Liam was right about his escape, though, it had been amazing. *Amazingly awful* – a dying father, a piece of paper pressed into his hand, and his father's last word, *Yours.*

He reached for the glass of whiskey and finished it off.

A piece of paper with a string of numbers scrawled across it - Dylan had known exactly what it was, an account number at Credit Suisse, the bank his father had deposited money into just hours before he'd died. His share of the business Big Jack Dunstan was trying to sell out from under him, he'd said.

The one thing that wasn't surprising in all of this, was that Dunstan had not forgotten about the money, not in all these years, not for one minute, for all the good it was going to do him. He didn't owe Jack Dunstan anything.

Not so with his father's youngest son.

"If I'd known about you, Liam, I'd have gotten you out of Georgia a long time ago." That was the best he could come up with, but he meant every word. Even at fifteen, he would have burned Georgia to the ground to save his brother from Margot and Big Jack Dunstan.

"I managed," the kid said.

"According to Tommy, you managed quite a few times."

"I gave him a run for his money," the kid agreed,

sitting back in his chair and crossing his arms over his chest.

"Until last night," Dylan said.

Another smile curved the boy's mouth. "Last night I gave him a run for *your* money, big brother. Five million dollars of your money sitting in a bank account at Credit Suisse with my name on it."

At the other end of the table, Hawkins choked on his cake.

CHAPTER THIRTEEN

LIAM DIDN'T TAKE HIS GAZE off his brother. He couldn't. For all his wild imaginings, Dylan Hart was not what he'd expected – not in any way.

The guy looked like him, shockingly so, but with another three inches in height, at least thirty more pounds of solid muscle, and a look in his eyes that said all the years Liam had spent playing *Call of Duty*, this man had been living it. And like everyone else Liam had met at Steele Street, his big brother had the worldwide lockdown on the word "calm." Steady. Solid. Like a rock. In no way was Dylan Hart the wild freebooter he'd thought he'd find. Not a con man. Not a hustler who'd outfoxed Big Jack.

And sure as hell, he was no car salesman.

He was a man to be reckoned with – and Skeeter and Hawkins knew it even more than he did. He'd seen the subtle deference inherent in their attention to Dylan. His big brother was the boss, the captain of this crew of badass boys and girls.

Jeez.

"So, you know about the money," his brother said.

Liam nodded. "It's the only thing Big Jack ever talks about when he's drinking, and he drinks a lot. He even took me to Geneva when I was sixteen, tried to pass me off as you to every bank in town. But no one had ever heard of Liam Dylan Magnuson – until we got to

Credit Suisse. While Jack was arguing with the banker, I wandered off, and this guard comes over to me, an older guy, looks me square in the eye and says, *"You are too young to be this man you claim to be. Go home before you get arrested."* So right then, bingo, I knew it was all true. The five million, and probably more by then, was sitting in Credit Suisse, and you were probably still out there, somewhere."

"And you never mentioned this to Jack?"

"Never once in my entire life have I ever mentioned *anything* to Jack," he said. "In fact, I have done my damnedest to stay as far away from Big Fat Daddy Jack as humanly possible."

To Liam's surprise, his comment got him a laugh – not much of one, but definitely a laugh.

"Well, you're right. Our father put five million into a Credit Suisse investment account in my name, in your name, just before he died," his brother said, returning to the subject at hand. "It's worth a bit more today."

Liam nodded.

"Half of it's yours."

Uh, no. No friggin' way.

Liam shook his head. "No, thanks." The last thing he wanted was to hang that damn money around his neck and spend the rest of his life worrying about who was coming up behind him, ready to wax his ass. Besides, he'd proven pretty damn good at making his own money. "No," he said. "I don't need your money."

"And I don't need yours." His brother was succinct.

Liam nodded without agreeing to anything. "It's not the reason I came looking for you, the money. Is there... uh...someplace where we could talk privately?"

Without hesitation, his brother rose from the table, taking his glass and picking up the bottle of Stranahan's.

Liam retrieved his backpack and biting back a soft groan, grabbed a glass for himself. It had been a long couple of days since he'd left Chicago, and he had some rough edges and plenty of aches and pains he'd like to smooth out. Personal experience told him whiskey might do the trick.

CHAPTER FOURTEEN

———

AT A PRIVATE AIRFIELD SOUTH of Denver, Big Daddy Jack Dunstan hoisted his considerable bulk into the shotgun seat of a black Lincoln Navigator, all the while struggling to catch his breath.

"Where's my damn oxygen?" he asked when he could finally get the words out. *Goddamn Denver didn't have much air in its goddamn air.*

Owen, one of the two men loading guns and gear into the back of the Navigator, reached into the backseat and retrieved a portable oxygen concentrator for him. Gus, the other man, kept loading their gear in the back.

Daddy Jack checked the flow on the concentrator and fitted the tubing to his face. It took a few good breaths before he started feeling better, like he wasn't going to goddamn die before he even got this show on the road.

He heard the SUV's lift gate close at the rear of the vehicle.

"Seven thirty-eight Steele Street," he said when Gus got in behind the wheel.

Gus and Owen were his handpicked "A" team, a matched set of shaved-head ball-busters, both of them built like slabs of granite. They were the best hunters he had - and no mistake, this was a hunting expedition, pure and simple.

"Got it, Big Jack," Gus said, pulling up the Navigator's GPS screen.

Twenty-three years. Jack had waited too damn long for this payday. Too damn long for that damn, thieving little bastard to raise his head long enough to get a bead on him.

But, by God, they had a bead on him now. All thanks to Robert Crandall Jr. of Crandall & Ellis LLP, a New York City law firm. One damn letter sent from Crandall Jr. to Liam Dylan Magnuson in Georgia four days ago, and the dominoes had started falling into place. Starting with Big Jack opening the letter no matter whose damn name was on it, to sending Tommy to Chicago with a copy of the letter to pick up the pansy-assed guitar player, to the guitar player making a run for it and leading them to the goddamn prize of the century - one damn domino after another, until the last one had hit pay dirt right here in goddamn Denver.

Nothing could have surprised him more.

All these years, he'd been convinced the money was in Switzerland. But no matter how many lawsuits he'd filed, or how many Georgia congressmen he'd sicced on those damn Swiss bankers, he'd never gotten a damn dime out of the place. He'd even taken little Liam once, tried to pass him off as the older boy, and gotten nowhere. It had all made him wonder if the money was even there. But if it wasn't in Geneva, where the hell was it?

New York City.

According to the letter, Big Jack's long dead business partner had stashed the older boy's "inheritance" in New York City with Crandall & Ellis, and those bastards were waiting for Liam Dylan Magnuson to come and get it.

Jack could A-1 guarantee that was going to happen – pronto.

Yes, sir, the smartest thing he'd ever done was convince Margot to give her second boy the same name as the first. To carry on the tradition, he'd told her, but he'd always been thinking that if he ever had a chance at the money, well, by God, he wanted to have a Liam Dylan Magnuson to go claim it.

And wouldn't you know it. The damn money had shown up, and Jack had not one, but two Liam Dylan Magnusons, and he was going to break whichever one he got his hands on first and drag him to New York to claim the inheritance Crandall & Ellis LLP had lost track of for over two decades. And then he was going to turn around and sue the bastard lawyers for keeping the money for so damn long. His money, no matter whose damn name was on it.

All these years, he'd thought the kid had gotten away with the money. He'd thought the kid had been so damn smart.

He'd been wrong. The kid had always been just a damn kid, while Crandall & Ellis LLP had been negligent beyond belief.

It was going to cost them.

"For my son, Liam Dylan Magnuson III," the letter had said. *"His inheritance, his patrimony, to be given to no other claimant."* The inheritance given to Attorney Robert Crandall Sr. by Liam Dylan Magnuson II twenty-three years ago for safekeeping. Given, and then forgotten when there'd been no Liam Dylan Magnuson III to be found. When Crandall Sr. had died recently, Crandall Jr. had found the Magnuson inheritance file in his father's papers and instigated a new search using the internet.

It hadn't taken the young attorney long to come up with a band named Never Celeste, fronted by Liam Magnus, a.k.a. Liam Dylan Magnuson.

Liam's inheritance? Jack had thought, reading the letter. Not very damn likely. That damn five million, plus interest, plus damages, and anything else he found at the attorneys' office belonged to Jack. He didn't give a damn about the "no other claimant." He had lawyers, too, lots of lawyers.

And today of all days, he was done screwing around. An hour before he and his team had gotten on the plane, he'd received a phone call. His trading partner in Atlanta had called to let him know the deal they'd been working on for the last four months had suddenly and inexplicably fallen through. Ted Patton of Patton Equipment, Inc. had walked away from the table. Gone, just like that. No reason given.

Ironically, just when he needed an infusion of cash more than ever, he was closer to his long-lost millions than he'd ever been.

He shifted in his seat to look over his shoulder at Owen. "Call the boys. Let 'em know we're here and to back off whatever the hell they've been up to."

"Yes, sir."

"Tell 'em they're going in with us to nab the old bastard."

"Old bastard, sir?"

"The first son. The older brother Liam," Jack grumbled. Nate packed a helluva punch, and that damn Bobby Lee had shot the guitar hero in the leg. Dragging a beaten-up cripple with him back east and propping him up in front of a bunch of New York City lawyers was too risky, looked too damn fishy, was too much like the Geneva fiasco. So, the smart move was to go for the real deal first. That bastard was kicking forty in the back and was no match for the juggernaut heading his way - Gus, Owen, and Big Jack Dunstan in the flesh.

He allowed himself a grin. Oh, yeah, that bastard's day of reckoning had come. Big Daddy Jack was heading toward him like a Cruise missile on overdrive.

CHAPTER FIFTEEN

LIAM WINCED AS HE EASED into one of the leather chairs grouped around a coffee table at the far end of the loft. His brother's home took up the entire top floor of the building and getting across it had just about taken his last ounce of energy. His head throbbed, his arm ached, and his gunshot wound simply hurt like hell.

"We can do this in the morning, if you want," his brother said.

"No. Now is good." He set his backpack on the table, determined to do what he'd come to do. The road to get here had been long and hard, almost the least of it what he'd endured last night.

He unzipped the pack's main compartment and took out seven well-worn paperback books and put them on the table – adventure stories, tales of derring-do and treasure, of survival, of boys and dogs striking out on their own and conquering the wilderness.

"All these books are from the bookshelves in my room, which I eventually figured out must have been your room before it was mine, and there are a couple of themes here," he said.

His brother picked up one of the books and let out a short laugh. "Every boy a hero, and every dog."

"And books you loved enough to read more than once. In some cases" – Liam lifted a book held together with a rubber band off the table – "a book you read until

it fell apart. That's what caught my eye, and I figured, hell, if my long-lost brother loved this book so much, maybe I ought to read it."
"*Call of the Wild*," his brother said.
"Yeah. Great story. I ended up reading it a few times myself, and every time, I kept coming back to this."
He slipped the rubber band off the book and handed the stack of loose pages to Dylan.
"If you look inside the front cover, you'll see a "This Book Belongs To" stamp and beneath it are three handwritten initials – L. D. M. Those are my initials, and they were yours, but then someone has crossed out the initials and put their own name in the book, and he did the same in all these books."
Liam watched his brother's gaze run down the length of the page to the name.
"Dylan Hart."
"Yeah," Liam said. "That guy. And so I was always wondering, who was this kid who was screwing around in me and my big brother's room, writing his name in our books? Who in the hell was this kid, Dylan Hart?"

Who in the hell, indeed? Dylan thought.
It took a helluva lot to startle him, but Liam just had, in spades.
Geezus. All those years of stealing cars and hiding out in Denver, he'd been one Jack London novel away from being found. Or rather – he glanced over the books on the table – two Jack London novels and five other adventure books, everything from *Dogsong*, to *Hatchet*, to *Treasure Island* and *Kidnapped*, all of them in a room Jack Dunstan had walked past every day.
He sat back in his chair, listening as Liam continued,

watching him speak and gesture and pretty much all-around confound and amaze.

"Then one night, while Big Jack was bitching about the money, drunk as usual," Liam was saying, "he said the damnedest thing, had probably said it hundreds of times, but I was never listening. That night, he said the only way that damn, smart-ass kid could have gotten out of Switzerland without him knowing it, was if that kid had changed his damn name."

Indeed, Dylan thought. It had been the only way.

"At first," Liam said, "I was only thinking what a great idea that was. That I'd have better luck running away and not getting caught, if I changed my name, too." He reached out and picked up one of the books. "So, I got to thinking about a new name for myself. It could be anything, right? But it had to be cool, something easy to remember. And then, there it was." He opened the front cover of *Treasure Island* and showed the inside to Dylan. "Right in front of me my whole life – Dylan Hart."

He let out a short laugh and put the book back on the table.

"Trust me," he said, lifting his gaze, "it was about half a second from that thought to knowing that if you were still out there in the world, that's who you were, Dylan Hart."

And so he was.

Geezus.

"It was a comfort," Liam said, reaching out and pouring himself a short shot. "Finally knowing your name."

"How old were you?"

"Fifteen," he said, then tossed back the whiskey, finishing it in one swallow.

"But you didn't try to find me." The kid was obviously resourceful. He could have given it a go.

"No." Liam reached for his backpack. "No one had

heard from you in forever, not even Mom. You could have been dead, and I...uh, wasn't ready for that. It was better not to know anything, than to know that."

Dylan silently swore, feeling his control of the situation slip for reasons that had nothing and everything to do with the kid – and their mother. *Mom,* he had called her. But since Dylan had been fifteen, she'd only ever had one name to him – and he'd done his damnedest to forget even that one.

———

Cruising into downtown Denver, Big Jack twisted around to glare at Owen in the backseat of the Lincoln. "What do you mean those dumbass kids aren't answering their phones?"

"I've tried all three of them, Jack." Owen shrugged. "Left a message for Tommy to call, and one for Nate. Figured there was no sense in leaving a message for Ratface Raynor."

"Dumbass kids," Jack muttered. "How close are we, Gus?"

"Ten minutes out."

"Don't waste your breath calling again. Text. That's all these idiots do anymore," Jack said. "Text Tommy. He's supposed to be in charge. Let him know we're ten minutes out. He can wrangle the other two, get their asses in the Escalade, and get them to Steele Street."

"Yes, boss." Owen typed the message and hit send – and almost immediately got a reply. "They're on their way, Jack."

"About goddamn time."

———

Lieutenant Loretta pocketed Tommy's phone and turned to Weismann and the other assembled officers. "Saddle up, boys. This party is on."

CHAPTER SIXTEEN

———

MARGOT.
Their mother.

Dylan put the Jack London book back on the table, then slid his gaze to the bottle of whiskey.

At seventeen, he'd almost drank himself into a coma one night, trying to forget the last time he'd heard his mother's voice. It had taken her four days after his father had died to call. Three days after Jack and his goons had arrived and started putting the squeeze on him.

"Now honey, I'm telling you, stop whatever you're up to and get back to the hotel. Jack and his friends are still in Geneva. They're looking all over for you, worried sick. I don't know why in the world you would have run off, just being stubborn, as usual. Jack flew all the way there to take care of you, bring you home, but you have got to tell him where the money is. He knows your father took it, bless his soul, but that money belongs to Jack now, to the business – and we...we need it. So don't give me any sass and get back to the hotel. Or call Jack, and he'll come get you."

Dylan had known that last bit for a fact. Jack and his crew had been tearing through Geneva, trying to find him, and it had taken everything Dylan had to keep ahead of the bastards. He'd been living on the razor's edge and on the run for three days, fifteen years old, lost, and flat-out scared to death that if he didn't move fast enough, wasn't smart enough, someone was going to drag him out of the darkness of his grief and kill him. He'd been right.

He'd thought Big Jack was coming to Geneva to help him get his father's body home, to take care of the million things that had crashed down on him when his father had collapsed with a heart attack and died – but Jack hadn't come to help him.

Jack had come to help himself. He'd come for the money. The only thing standing in his way was finding out where it was, and getting rid of anyone else who might have a claim, like the boy whose name was the same as the man's who'd taken the money - Liam Dylan Magnuson.

And last night, Tommy Dunstan and two of his thugs had descended on his brother with the same evil intent for the same damn money – to torture and coerce Liam, until what? Until they went too far?

Leaning forward, Dylan poured himself and Liam another shot, and he wondered if he'd be feeling more settled if he'd slammed Tommy Dunstan into the wall a couple of times - hard.

Probably, he decided. Probably would have done both him and Tommy a lot of good.

"But then Tommy shows up with this," Liam said, rustling around in the backpack before pulling out an envelope. He held it in his hands for a moment, then handed it across the table. "Whatever Dad left you is with these lawyers in New York, and when I read it, I... uh, knew I didn't have any more excuses. I had to find you. You had to know."

Dylan took the letter out of the envelope, and paused, his attention shifting briefly to Hawkins at the far side of the room. His second-in-command held up three fingers with one hand and lifted a phone in the other, then turned and headed back toward the dining room.

Got it. Message received: Dunstan had been spotted

on Steele Street. He had two guys with him. And if Dylan so wanted, he could monitor the building's security cameras on his phone.

Dylan returned his attention to the letter, noticed it was a copy, which verified what Tommy had told him, then quickly skimmed the contents. *Inheritance, patrimony* – the letter was brief and did not specifically mention money. Tommy and Big Jack Dunstan were on a fool's errand.

And it was going to cost them everything.

"Jack's a crazy sonuvabitch," Liam said. "I saw him put his fist through a window once, trying to prove what he was going to do to you, if he ever got his hands on you." Another of those small grins curved the kid's mouth. "But I don't think he has a clue who he's up against." His grin widened as he slowly shook his head. "Not one...single...clue."

Smart kid.

Whatever was going to happen with Jack Dunstan wasn't going to get past Creed and Hawkins, and wasn't going to get anywhere near the thirteenth floor and Liam. On the other hand, Dunstan's crew wouldn't have much trouble breaking into the building from the alley and racking up another felony. Creed had made sure of it. And to keep everything on the up-and-up, Lieutenant Loretta had stationed a couple of Denver's finest near Steele Street and 17th Avenue, in case Dunstan had brought some firepower to make good on the plan he'd texted Tommy - *I'm on my way, and we'll blow this bastard right out of his rat hole.*

Not this bastard, Dylan thought, *and not this rat hole.*

He slipped his phone out of his pocket, turned it on, and set it on the edge of the table, angling it away from Liam. The kid was half asleep and had been through enough in the last twenty-four hours. Anything he wanted to see, Dylan would play for him tomorrow.

For tonight, he was done.

But the night wasn't over yet. Two taps on his phone got Dylan what he wanted, a split screen showing both ground level entrances to 738 Steele Street – a massive set of mahogany doors leading to an elegant lobby, and a windowless, ironclad door in a dark alley next to an old freight elevator.

Liam leaned forward and tossed back the shot of whiskey, then settled into his chair. "So," he said. "What is it you guys do here? Private SWAT team for hire? Mercenaries? Your own personal army?"

"Government task force." A simple explanation for a complicated situation.

"Our government?" Liam asked, a quizzical expression on his face, as if he wasn't quite sure whether or not he was ready for the answer.

Dylan spared him any confusion.

"Yes." One word, short, succinct, and without question, the end of this particular conversation.

Liam got the message loud and clear.

"Alrighty, then, tell me about Dad."

Fair enough.

"You would have been his favorite, hands down."

"Not even," the boy scoffed, then grinned. "Really? You think?"

Dylan didn't think it. He knew it. "Dad had a musical streak, played piano. He was pretty good, always wished he had the time to get better, and he'd be so proud of you. He'd have been your biggest fan."

"Cool." The boy nodded slowly. "Very cool. I play piano, too, and guitar a little, here and there, but mostly I sing."

That was one way to put it, Dylan thought. He'd also looked the kid up on the internet, and honestly, had been blown away that he could have anything genetically in common with anyone with as much talent and artistry as Liam Magnus.

"And you know..." Liam yawned. "You know this is crazy, right? You and me sitting here. This whole crazy lawyer thing bringing us together."

"Crazy," Dylan agreed, figuring the kid had less than five minutes before the alcohol and exhaustion knocked him out

Liam yawned again and relaxed deeper into his chair.

"You'd think it would be impossible to miss someone you never knew, but I always missed him."

Yeah, Dylan missed him, too.

"So how'd you come up with the name Dylan Hart?"

"Well, no offense to either of us," Dylan said, "or Dad, or Granddad, but I always thought Liam Dylan Magnuson III sounded more like a fussy old Scottish lord than a guy who could survive on his own in the wilds of Alaska. So, I took our middle name and added an Old English word for a stag. That was the coolest thing I could think of when I was ten." An explanation, he realized, he might have to give again. Liam had dozed off.

Twenty-two years old.

Beat to crap.

And done for the night.

A flicker of light drew his attention back to his phone.

Dunstan and his two guys were at Steele Street's front door, and Dylan had to say, Jack Dunstan looked like he could keel over any minute. Three hundred pounds of old man hauling around an oxygen machine, backed up by a couple of generic, shaved-head knuckle-draggers. They rattled the handles, shoved on the doors, and then noticed the sign Creed had posted just for them – *Deliveries Accepted In Alley.*

It was like waving a dead chicken in front of a pack of hyenas.

The knuckle-draggers looked around at all the people

and cars passing by on Steele Street and took the bait, heading to the alley with Jack bringing up the rear.

They were out of camera range for a little over a minute before they showed up in front of the iron door in the alley. Under the cover of darkness, the two thugs broke the cheap padlocks Creed had put on the door. When Jack caught up to them, everyone pulled out their pistols and all three men entered the ground floor of Steele Street.

Police cruiser lights instantly flashed across the upper screen on Dylan's phone, heading into the alley. Almost immediately, more cruiser lights flashed on the lower screen, coming from the other end of the alley. Within seconds, a couple of explosions went off in the ground floor garage – flash-bangs, compliments of Creed - and the knuckle-draggers stumbled back out the alley door into the waiting arms of Denver's finest.

Game over.

The perfect take-down.

Not a shot fired.

With Jack Dunstan finally lumbering out like a beached whale to complete the deal.

"So, Dylan Hart," Liam said, coming around a bit. His voice was soft, and a little slurred by the whiskey.

Dylan looked over at him. The kid's eyes were barely open.

"*Call of the Wild,* Dylan Hart," his brother said, "where do we go from here?"

"I say we go to New York, see these lawyers, and find out what Dad left us." Dylan didn't have a clue what it might be.

A sleepy smile curved the boy's mouth. "And after that?"

"Forward, little brother," he said. "We go forward from there."

CHAPTER SEVENTEEN

―――◆―――

Seven months later, February, The Canyon Club, Denver, Colorado

A FIVE-PIECE HARD ROCK BAND ROCKING hard was about two more pieces than The Canyon Club could really handle. Dylan's earplugs needed earplugs. He was jammed up against the back wall and the bar, next to Hawkins, Katya, and Travis. All around them, the crowd seethed, shouted, sweated, everyone fixated on the stage and the tattooed, raspy-voiced frontman wailing into the microphone. The kid had range, four octaves of it, hitting notes up and down the scale from a low growl to a primal scream to the melodies in between.

Dylan's forays onto the internet had not done the boy justice. His little brother was electric on stage. Born to rule. Liam Magnus wasn't a singer. He was a Rock Star. It poured off him. Washed over the crowd. Pulled all of them into the palm of his hand – or anywhere else he wanted to take them. A driving bass line alongside the lead guitarist with a Les Paul, rhythm guitarist running a Stratocaster, and a maniac on the drums backed the kid up and fueled the mayhem of Never Celeste.

For sheer overkill, the band had two very beautiful, very tough-looking, girl dancers, stage names Hell & Fury – a.k.a Red Dog and Skeeter, making it family night at The Canyon Club. All Dylan could say was that women who were incredibly fit could dance incredibly well. He was seeing moves he hadn't seen before, which got him to thinking the things he was usually thinking when he thought about the blonde. He hoped she didn't wear herself out too much by dancing half the night.

Hawkins leaned in close. "The girls have got themselves some serious moves," he shouted.

Dylan nodded. Serious moves – shaking, twisting, undulating, totally synchronized, both of them in black bustiers and pirate masks, with black-sequined, ultra-mini skirts that barely hung onto their hips when they shimmied.

Talk about electrifying. It drove the audience crazy when they shimmied.

At Thanksgiving, when Liam had come home for the holiday, they'd pushed and wheedled and damn near begged him to let them dance on stage when he and the band previewed their new songs in Denver. At Christmas, when Liam had come home for the holiday, they'd pushed some more, sealing the deal by showing off the routines they'd put together. Needless to say, Liam had capitulated. The girls rocked, and Dylan had to admit it was wonderful to see his hardworking, kick-ass, badass girls do something just for the fun of it. Thank God neither of them could carry a tune, or little brother might have offered them a job. The crowd loved them almost as much as he personally loved the phrase "when Liam had come home for the holiday."

Yeah, he and little brother had something going on. Just when Dylan had thought his heart was already full.

Go figure.

And now, the week before Valentine's, Liam had come home again.

"I've got moves," he said back to Hawkins, in case his second-in-command had any doubts. Maybe not dance moves, but he had moves.

"Ha!" Hawkins laughed out loud. "If you had a move, boss, I'd have seen it by now. Come on, babe," he leaned down to Katya, who was doing a little bump and grind in front of him. "Let's show the boss some moves."

Even with damn little floor space to work with, Katya definitely had moves. She turned and flowed into Superman's arms, taking hold of his hand, her shoulders shaking, her hips keeping rhythm with her husband's, the two of them dirty-dancing like they were born to it.

On the other side of Hawkins, Dylan caught Travis's gaze, and the Angel boy grinned – and started his own move, pushing into the crowd, hips swaying as he slip-slided through all those gyrating bodies.

No one should have been able to get through that mass of people, but Travis moved like he was moving through water, drifting with the tide, which eventually washed him up on the shore. One-handed, he lofted himself onto the stage. When Liam shoved the microphone in his direction, he took the time to face-off with the Never Celeste frontman and sing the next line in the song, which got him a rousing cheer. Then he turned around and picked up one of the dancing girls, "Hell," throwing her over his shoulder and exiting stage right. The crowd went wild, and the band played louder.

Well, Dylan *definitely* wasn't doing that.

No, his girl knew where he was...and it appeared that Hawkins and Katya had dirty-danced their way right out the door.

Those two – *sheesh*. Three kids already, and gunning for a fourth.

Dylan returned his attention to the stage. Liam was wearing a black leather vest embroidered with the Never Celeste logo, a pair of black pants, no shirt, black boots, and their grandfather's Rolex Explorer, the watch their father had left with Crandall & Ellis in New York for his son.

That had turned into a helluva trip. Liam had a lot of friends in New York, and Dylan had seen a side of the city that had been...well, a helluva lot of fun.

He grinned. He was taking Skeeter next week, for Valentine's, and letting Liam play tour guide to the Big Apple's underground art and music scene.

Life was good.

And getting better. "Fury" danced her way off the stage, making a beeline toward him, and the crowd parted like the Red Sea, which said something about the power of a beautiful blonde with a platinum ponytail hanging halfway down her back and a lightning bolt tattoo shooting up her leg and over her shoulder.

His woman.

She'd cornered him one night on the Mother Margot situation, now that they had Liam in their lives. Not a situation, he'd assured her, and it wasn't. He wasn't angry anymore. He wasn't anything when it came to Margot — except grateful to have a brother. With Jack Dunstan buried in lawyers, felonies, and bankruptcy, Liam was financially supporting her, and even that was more than Dylan needed to know. He'd cut the apron strings long before he'd torched the maternal bridge on that cold and heartless night in Geneva. The bond he'd formed with Hawkins and the rest of the crew at sixteen had held him close. Had held him tight.

It still did.

But no one held him tighter than the woman moving in on him with her own shimmy, shimmy, bump and grind. With every move she made, the crowd pushed back, the better to watch her dance. A couple of guys started to reach for her.

And that's when Dylan made his move.

It was his best move.

The one he was good at.

No hip shaking.

No shoulder shimmy.

Just one solid step forward with his arm going around her waist and pulling her in close, pulling her in tight, taking care of business, taking care of his own.

That was his move – always. Taking care of his own.

"Hey, baby." Skeeter wrapped her arms around his neck and kissed his cheek.

He kissed her back. "You have fun tonight?"

"Not as much fun as I'm going to have," she said, giving him a little shake of her hips.

He laughed and gathered her in closer. "I've got a car waiting out front. Is Grady spending the night at Creed and Cody's?"

"Not tonight. The plan was after they put the twins to bed, Creed would take Grady up to our place and get him all snugged in. I'm sure that happened hours ago, and Creed's just waiting for us to get home."

And all would be safe – and quiet. Creed sipping a little whiskey and watching the night and the city lights. Grady couldn't have better care.

Special Defense Force, SDF, was an elite team of soldiers, tasked by the United States government to protect the country from threats both near and far – and so they did, time and time again.

But long before they'd been soldiers, they'd been brothers, lost boys who had banded together to survive, sworn to protect each other - and so they do.

All the time.

Every time.

H ELLO DEAR READERS! A few years back, I was honored to be asked to write a short story for inclusion in SEAL OF MY DREAMS, an anthology with a triple purpose: to honor the men and women in our nation's military; to raise money for Veterans Research Corporation, a non-profit foundation supporting veterans medical research – all proceeds from the sale of the anthology went to the foundation; and to entertain readers with great stories about Navy SEALs. Eighteen romance writers answered the call. PANAMA JACK, with a tie-in to Steele Street, was the story I donated. Had a blast writing it. Hope you enjoy!

 xoxo

PANAMA JACK

TARA JANZEN

ONE

Darien Gap, Panama

"YOU'VE GOT THAT LOW-CRAWL DOWN real good, ma'am, very fine action on the move. Very fine, indeed." Panama Jack Corday had a reputation for calling 'em like he saw 'em, and the girl wiggling up next to him in this godforsaken jungle had a backside worthy of worship.

"Watch yourself, Flipper," she said, handing him an MRE—Meal Ready to Eat—and settling back into her rifle. "I've got enough trouble without you getting all worked up staring at my derrière."

She also had a mouth on her. Flipper. Hell. Nobody had ever had the guts to call him Flipper, but she did it regularly. Her little way of trying to keep him in line, he guessed.

Fat chance.

He grinned. "I love it when you talk dirty."

"Derrière?" She slanted him a quick glance over the top of her rifle. "That's not dirty, it's French."

"Dirty French." His grin broadened.

"*In your dreams,*" she said under her breath, resting her cheek back on the rifle's stock and peering through the scope.

She had that right—*in his dreams.* Hell, if he'd had a night in the last two months when she hadn't been in his dreams, he didn't remember it. Oh, hell, no. Little Miss Blondie with the O.G.A., Other Government Agency, a.k.a. the C.I.A., had been popping in and out of Panama City on a damn near weekly basis, and every week she requested one operator to take her deep into the overgrown danger zone between Panama and Colombia known as the Darien Gap. Every week she requested him, Jack Corday, U.S. Navy SEAL on special assignment.

Special assignment to cover Little Miss Blondie's very fine derrière. *Yeah,* he'd finally figured it out.

But he hadn't figured her out.

He opened up the package of cookies in the MRE and handed her a couple, then put his eye back to the spotting scope and scanned the area in front of them.

Nothing about the Ice Queen made sense. She was half spook, half sniper, and all gorgeous. Agents like her usually ended up in European embassies, carrying a pocket pistol and collecting intelligence from tuxedoed diplomats.

This girl was in the middle of the big, bad nowhere, sweating her guts out and toting a M40, a fully accurized .308 with a scope that cost more than his first car.

"So, do you ever take a day off?" Yep, that was him, all right, a real smooth guy.

"Not in this lifetime," she said dryly.

"Maybe you should try it, with me."

"Maybe not." Without an instant's hesitation, she turned him down, but he was a U.S. Navy SEAL and SEALs never gave up. Never.

"I could take you fishing." He was good at fishing.

Her little snort of derision implied that fishing might be a long shot.

Grinning, he popped the last cookie into his mouth and glanced over at her. "If you'd tell me what you're looking for, maybe I could help you find it." After eight times of getting dropped into this hellhole and bushwhacking their way to the same damn hillside to stare down at the same damn abandoned farmhouse, and getting nowhere doing it, he figured she might be ready for a little professional guidance.

He'd figured wrong.

"That's real sweet of you, Squidbreath," she said, keeping her gaze focused through the scope and for damn sure looking like she knew what she was doing. "But if I told you what I'm looking for, I'd have to kill you."

He grinned again, and checked his watch. *Squidbreath?*

"We're running out of time," he told her. "We need to get to the LZ." If all had gone according to plan, the helo designated to pick them up was on its way.

"Five more minutes," she said. "Then we'll pack it in, which means we'll be right back here doing this again next week."

That was all right by him. He'd had worse missions, far worse than being teamed up with Little Miss Blondie.

"So when are you going to tell me your name?" he asked.

"You know my name."

"Oh, yeah, Smith, Jane Smith," he recalled. "Or was it Johnson? Jane Johnson?"

"I always heard SEALs were real smart," she said. "You got it right the first time. Smith Jane Smith."

"So should I be calling you Smith or Jane?"

"You can keep calling me what you've been calling me—'Yes, ma'am.'"

She had that right. He'd been "Yes, ma'aming," Little Miss Blondie from the moment they'd met.

"Two o'clock," she whispered, going very still next to him on the jungle floor.

Yeah, he heard it, too, the soft cough of an engine coming off the mountain pass north of the abandoned farm. He angled the spotting scope in that direction, following the winding path of the dirt road up through the trees until he saw an old deuce-and-a-half lumbering toward the valley below.

"Delivery time?" he asked.

"I sure as hell hope so," she said, and for the first time, he detected an honest, unguarded emotion in her voice—naked anticipation. She wanted this, whatever "this" was. It could be anything, weapons, drugs, a squad of narco-guerillas. For sure, it would be trouble.

"You've got a plan for whatever comes out of that truck, right?"

"Right." She nestled in closer to her rifle.

"Want to tell me what it is, in case I need to step in and save the day?"

"You just keep doing what you're doing, Corday, and everything will be just fine."

Oh, man, he could hardly believe the size of her *cojones*. But when he'd been given this assignment, his commanding officer had made it crystal clear that he was going to be working for "Jane Smith," not the other way around. She called the shots. She gave the orders, and he got her where she wanted to go and got her back out.

The minutes ticked by in silence, both of them watching the truck slowly rumble its way down the gullies and over the rocks in the road. Sweat ran down his face. Doubt edged into his mind. Wasn't it just like a damn C.I.A. agent to drag him into something without telling him what in the hell was going on? PSD, he'd been told, a Personal Security Detail. But who in the world ever did a PSD for a fricking sniper?

No one, that's who.

The truck started across the valley, heading for the farmhouse. When it reached the path leading to the adjoining, ramshackle barn, it stopped. A man wearing jungle boots and camouflage got out of the cab and headed around to the back of the deuce-and-a-half, no doubt getting ready to unload whatever it was Smith was hoping to score.

Jack did a quick mental check of all his gear, which most definitely included an M4 carbine and a .45 caliber pistol with plenty of extra magazines for both. He was ready. He was always ready.

But nothing came out of the back of the truck—no drugs, no weapons, no narco-guerillas. The driver kicked the tires, checked a load strap, looked at the farm and empty pastures for a few seconds, then came back around to the front of the truck, got into the cab, and started up the deuce. The engine sputtered and coughed, and finally turned over a couple of times, and then it died.

Jack didn't move, not so much as a muscle twitch. Beside him, Smith had gone pure mannequin, her gaze glued to the scope, her breathing so soft as to be damn near imperceptible.

Down below, the driver gave another long go of cranking the engine, and just when Jack was thinking it was time for the guy to give up, the old truck roared to life. Mission accomplished—or maybe not. Next to him, he caught the slight movement of Smith's finger sliding onto the trigger.

The driver sure as hell had screwed up something, and it was going to cost him his life. At four hundred meters with no wind, the girl wasn't going to miss. She'd been dialed in on the guy's location for the last five hours. But the truck didn't move, and she didn't shoot. Everybody was waiting for something, but he'd be damned if he knew what, until the driver reached out the window with a red rag in his hand and cleaned off the side mirror. Next to him, Smith eased her finger off the trigger. When the driver followed up the red rag with a bright yellow one, giving the outside mirror a real thorough polishing, she whispered one, succinct word.

"*Bingo.*"

She'd gotten what she wanted, and he knew it was more than just a clean mirror on some damn paramilitary deuce-and-a-half. A message had been passed, and Smith liked the news.

Down below, the driver finished with the mirror and started grinding the gears, looking for first. When he got it right, the truck took off with a lurch and a roll and continued down the valley.

Jack glanced over and caught Smith looking at him with a big, sweet grin on her face, a wide curve of soft lips, perfect white teeth, and so-help-him-God dimples that for a second turned him just a little bit inside out, but just for a second. Then he recovered.

Just in time for her to jerk his chain again.

"Are you ready to kick this game up a notch and have some fun?" she asked, her pale green eyes lit with excitement. Her grin broadened, deepening those so-help-him-God dimples, and all of a sudden he was just a little bit inside out again.

Oh, yeah, he silently answered. He was ready for just about anything with Little Miss Blondie, had been for weeks, and *oh, yeah,* he was in trouble here—real trouble.

"Born ready," he said with a curt nod, ignoring whatever emotion was getting all churned up in his chest. Or maybe whatever was getting churned up was a little farther down his anatomy. "But I'm damned curious about what just happened, and about what didn't happen. If the guy hadn't cleaned his mirror . . . " He let the question trail off.

"I had him in my crosshairs with a half pound of pressure on a two-and-a-half pound trigger," she said, confirming exactly what he'd thought. "If he wasn't my messenger boy, then we'd been compromised, and he was a bad guy in the wrong place at the wrong time."

Good enough for Jack—and he was impressed as hell. He liked working with people who knew what it took to get the job done and get out in one piece.

"So what have you got in mind?" He was up for damn near anything.

"Drinks," she said. "At Las Palmas in Casco Viejo."

For a moment, all he could do was look at her, completely caught off guard. Weeks of ignoring him, and now she was asking him out for a drink? Highly trained operative that he was, he recovered quickly and gave her another nod.

"What time would you like to be picked up?" Having a drink together wasn't his *numero uno* hot, green-eyed blonde fantasy. In his *numero uno* fantasy, he and secret agent Jane Smith spent the night tearing up the sheets in the downtown bungalow where he always stayed , compliments of a buddy of his, J.T. Chronopolous. But she had definitely nailed the far distant number two or three spot on his current personal hit parade—Las Palmas, an elegant waterfront hotel in Panama City's historic district, Casco Viejo, drinks to start, maybe moving onto wine and dinner, and her, Little Miss Blondie, illuminated by candlelight without any visible firearms at the table.

But she was shaking her head.

"I'll meet you there, at midnight. I'll be bringing you a small gift, but don't feel obliged to return the favor. Just take a seat at the bar and order a drink. I'll come up and set my cigarette case down next to your glass. When I leave, pick up the case, and deliver it to Benjamin Neville's office at the U.S. Embassy, where we met. He'll be expecting you."

From bodyguard to delivery boy—she'd done it again,

caught him off guard and put him in his place.

"Yes, ma'am." Apparently, they'd gotten everything they'd come for, and he was ready to blow this pop stand, but she wasn't finished.

"How long have you been with the SEALs?" she asked, sizing him up, cool and steady with her green-eyed gaze. It didn't make him uncomfortable in the least. He knew who he was, and he could take all comers, including beautiful C.I.A. agents.

"Five years, ma'am."

"Seen a lot of action?"

"Some." A whole lot of "some." Iraq, Afghanistan, all over Central America, and a dozen other places, but somehow ending up in Panama enough that it felt like home. The surfing was great, the beer was cold, and every now and then something damned interesting landed in his lap—like Smith Jane Smith, a.k.a. Little Miss Blondie. Not that he'd be calling her that to her face anytime soon.

"I need you watching my back tonight in Casco Viejo," she said, her gaze still so cool and steady. "Get to the bar an hour before me and keep your eyes open."

"Yes, ma'am." Amazingly, not one lewd, smart-ass thought even went through his mind about watching her back or her backside. She was damned serious, and rightly so. Las Palmas was a classy place, but beyond its elegant walls, the neighborhood of Casco Viejo was dangerously sketchy after dark.

"Powell," she said, obviously coming to a decision about him. "Alanna Powell, but you can call me Lani." She stuck out her hand.

"Lani." He took her hand in his and gave it a firm shake, grinning. "Corday. Squidbreath Corday, but you can call me Flipper."

Her smile and her dimples returned, and there the two of them were, sweat-stained and mud-streaked, holding hands in the jungle and grinning like a couple of hormone-addled teenagers instead of two of Uncle Sam's finest and brightest.

Right in the nick of time to keep him from doing or saying anything too stupid, the sound of the helo coming in over the mountains broke the silence, and the two of them got to work. In less than a minute, they'd stowed their gear and were heading down the trail.

TWO

Casco Viejo, Panama City

SHE WAS LATE.

Lani stepped out of the smoke-filled Club Firenze and moved quickly across the cobblestone street, tucking a small silver case into the bodice of her mini-dress. Zebra-striped and strapless, the dress had a built-in underwire bra with a secret pocket for the case and enough spandex to fit her like a second skin. With her short blond hair spiked up, black leather cuffs on each wrist, big white hoop earrings, and a small black clutch purse slung over her shoulder she was perfectly camouflaged for the Panama City dance-club scene, equal parts urban-punk lion tamer and Sheba, Queen of the Jungle.

Behind her, hard rock music blared out of the packed club. Ahead of her, two blocks away, she could see Las Palmas, the pale stucco of its Spanish Colonial façade rising above the shops and restaurants clustered around the upper-end condominium buildings on the waterfront.

Casco Viejo was part slum, part construction site, part trendy tourist attraction, and no place for a *gringa* walking alone at midnight. But it wasn't the sullen-faced group of young men eyeing her from the corner that set her on edge. Oh, no. Her contact had done that quite nicely at their meeting.

A quick glance behind her proved Vasily Nikolayevich was still on the second-floor balcony of the club where she'd left him, watching her. Their meeting had gone longer than planned, with him stepping out twice to take a phone call, and Lani's unease had increased with every delay. She'd come to Panama to close a deal with Nikolayevich, a former KGB agent turned illegal arms dealer, a deal she'd been working on for over a year. In exchange for a substantial cash payment, and to put himself in the good graces of the U.S. government, should he ever need them, he had offered her a cigarette case electro-magnetically encrypted with the port designation, arrival date, and the BIC-Code of a shipping container transporting a load of shoulder-fired surface to air missiles, SAMs, destined for the Taliban from their comrades in arms, the Colombian guerillas known as the National Revolutionary Forces, the NRF—a deal guaranteed to fan the flames of the global war on terror.

Mission accomplished.

Except Nikolayevich had been two months late getting to Panama—two months he'd spent holed up in Colombian jungle with the damned NRF. Two months when her superiors had started to doubt the veracity of her information and her ability to get Nikolayevich to the table. Today, the tide had turned in her direction. The red flag at the farmhouse had told her Nikolayevich had finally crossed the border into Panama. The yellow flag had been the code for a meeting in Panama City.

And the sudden rising of the hair on the back of her neck told her she was being followed. It wasn't Nikolayevich. Grossly overweight and out of shape, he couldn't have fought his way through the crowd gyrating on the Club Firenze dance floor without giving himself a heart attack.

But there was a chance he had sold her out. He might not have come to Panama City alone. But neither had she. Lieutenant Jack Corday, U.S. Navy SEAL, nearly six feet of rock-hard brawn and Mensa caliber brains nicknamed Panama Jack, all of him honed and trained to a razor's edge of operational skill, was on her side.

And on her mind way too much since the first day he'd walked into Benjamin Neville's office at the U.S. Embassy and been introduced as her assigned escort. In his dress whites, he'd been impossible to ignore, dark-haired and blue-eyed, and so supremely self-assured that he'd just about broken her heart without doing a damn thing but stand there. When he'd flashed her a cocksure grin during their briefing, the deed had been done - *Yes, ma'am, I can take care of you, one hundred percent guaranteed.* Sure, she'd kept her cool, but a week later she'd made mistake number one: She'd requested him by name when she'd found herself back in Panama. He was irreverent and intelligent, and gorgeous, and hot, and interested, and so help her God, she knew better. Eight separate times, she'd known better, and eight separate times, when Benjamin Neville had asked who she wanted, she'd said Lieutenant Corday. She called him Squidbreath to keep herself in line, not him.

In five more steps, she reached the well-lit entryway of Las Palmas and passed under the pale pink arch into the luxurious hotel. Inside, crystal chandeliers cast a soft golden glow over marble floors and paneled teak walls. Without breaking her stride or looking anywhere except dead-ahead through the French doors leading to the bar, she pulled a cigarette case out of her purse and opened it. The case had a built-in lighter, and after selecting a cigarette and putting it between her lips, she stopped, seemingly by happenstance, next to a super-sized bouquet of tropical flowers and lit up. Cupping the flame, she inhaled, then blew out a long breath of smoke and with a slight flick of her wrist, dropped the case into the elaborate flower arrangement.

Whoever was following her was practically required by secret agent law to pillage the bouquet, giving her time to make the real drop in the bar, and that would be that. *Sayonara,* Navy SEAL. *Adios,* Corday. Goodbye, Flipper, and hello promotion. The lieutenant would head for the embassy, and she'd be on the next flight to Virginia.

Passing through the open glass doors, she picked him out of the crowd jamming the long, mahogany curve of the Las Palmas bar, and damn but the boy cleaned up good. Crisp, black T-shirt under a white suit jacket with black slacks, and swear to God, Italian leather loafers all but shouted "GQ." Add his chiseled jaw, deep-set blue eyes, the scar cutting across his left eyebrow, and that damn crooked grin of his, and all she could see was "Heartbreaker."

She wasn't the only one. A leggy redhead in tight gold pants and a green halter top was sidled up close to him, bending in close for Jack to light her cigarette. It was the perfect cover for the drop—and perfectly annoying.

Repressing a sigh, she worked her way up to the bar and leaned in next to him.

"Mojito," she called out to the bartender, flashing a twenty dollar bill she'd pulled out of her purse and completely ignoring the broad back she was brushing up against.

Sure she was.

She stubbed out her cigarette in the ashtray next to his beer. She needed a life. Something more than just a job that kept her on the road and on the run twelve months out of twelve. Honestly, she did.

Hell, for all she knew, she might like fishing.

Glancing back, she took note of the man digging through the tropical bouquet in the lobby—gray-haired and pock-marked and unquestionably Slavic. It had occurred to her more than once that the Russians might be keeping track of Nikolayevich, the same way they kept track of so many of their former comrades, especially those in the arms trade.

But this old guy didn't have a chance against her. Even at five feet, five inches and a hundred and twenty pounds she was one of the agency's big bad girls – and most of the time she had enough sense to stay away from the big bad boys. Why Corday was different, she didn't even want to know.

Her mojito came, and in between paying for it and pocketing her change, she slipped the silver cigarette case out of her bodice and set it next to Jack's beer with her hand covering it.

Or maybe all she needed was a vacation, just a little time off to recharge.

"Thanks, sugar," the redhead drawled on Jack's other side. "Or should I be saying *muchas gracias, azucar?*"

Despite her best efforts, Lani's damn annoyed sigh escaped her.

Squidbreath did not seem to notice.

"It's no problem, ma'am," he said. "I'm happy to help."

Lani didn't doubt it for a moment. Every guy she knew was happy to help redheads who were practically falling out of their halter tops.

"I like a helpful man," the redhead said, her voice a low, intimate purr. "Maybe we could get together later and party."

"Maybe we could, ma'am."

Oh, for crying out loud, Lani thought.

With the cigarette case on the bar between them, it was time for her to pick up her drink and wander off. Instead, in her estimation, and much to her irritation, Panama Jack was far too distracted by the redheaded woman to be left alone with the case. Damn Benjamin Neville for bringing a tradecraft rookie in on her mission, and why in the hell hadn't she noticed Lieutenant Corday's shortcomings earlier?

Because you spent too much time staring at his butt, Lani girl.

Well, hell. She couldn't deny it.

Stalling, she took a sip of the mojito and let her gaze drift across the mirror behind the bar - until it slammed into a black-eyed gaze locked onto her like a tractor beam, Alek Zhivkov, a.k.a. Zhivkov the Butcher. She swore one succinct word. She had ten rounds in an XDM Compact .45 in her purse, and if this deal got salty, his name was going on the one she kept in the chamber. Zhivkov had a long, sordid list of international crimes as a Russian Mafia enforcer, mostly in human trafficking, and she hated to see him branching out into her neck of the woods, illegal arms sales. As for Nikolayevich, if Zhivkov was checking up on him, she gave him a month on the outside, before he was dead.

It was time to run, and the smart money said she should take the case with her, but she no sooner closed her hand around it, than Corday's hand came around hers, holding onto her like he was never going to let her go.

Twenty minutes, Jack thought. That's how late she'd been getting to Las Palmas, twenty minutes of hell, and now she thought she was going to skip out on him?

He didn't think so. A minute ago, she could have left as planned. Thirty seconds ago, he might still have let her go, but not now, not under the current circumstances.

"Later then, sugar," the flirty redhead said, turning and walking away, thankfully at an angle that didn't impede his line of sight to the lobby.

Jack turned back to his beer, shifting his gaze to the

mirror to keep everyone in sight, including his hand-holding partner. The light in the bar was dim, but he still got an eyeful.

Zebra stripes. *Wow.* If he'd thought she looked good in muddy camos, Lani Powell flat-out owned him in a strapless, black and white-striped mini-dress, and here he was again, just a little bit upside down and inside out.

"You were followed," he said. Despite the redhead trying to distract him, he'd known the instant Lani had entered Las Palmas, and he'd known the instant she'd slipped in next to him at the bar, but he hadn't known that the bare curves of her shoulders and the upper curves of her breasts were so creamily, silkily beautiful, or that her skin had a golden glow. He hadn't known he had such a weakness for bad-girl make-up and leather cuff bracelets.

He had known he had a weakness for her, and the damned torturous twenty minutes he'd spent wondering where in the hell she was had proved it the hard way.

"Roger, that," she acknowledged.

"And the guy who followed you, the one lost in the flowers back in the lobby, has called in his reinforcements. The black-haired man coming in through the French doors and staring a hole in your back looks like rough trade, and the bald guy walking in from the rear of the bar is planning on cutting off your escape."

He saw her shift her gaze beyond the bar to the far corner of the room.

"Rough trade's name is Alek Zhivkov," she said, "also known as Zhivkov the Butcher. Baldy is Dmitri Yudin."

Somehow, her knowing all these guys didn't improve his mood.

"Anglo-Saxon jungle queen doing business with old-school Russians in the heart of Panama City, I guess that's what globalization is all about," he said, trying to keep the tightness out of his voice, and failing. "We can either fight our way out of here or give them what they want. How important is the silver case under your hand?"

"It's electro-magnetically encrypted with the BIC-code of a shipping container holding a load of stolen, third generation SAMs, French Mistral, Russian SA-18, and Stinger B missiles headed toward Afghanistan."

Fight to the death, then, dammit. Their deaths, not his, and sure as hell not hers, which meant run.

"There's a stairway on the balcony that leads to the rooftop restaurant, and—"

"A fire escape down the back of the hotel," she interrupted him.

Good, he thought. They'd both done their homework, and with enough speed, they should be able to get some distance on the Russians.

"You take the case, babe, and run like hell."

Smart girl, she didn't waste a second buying into his plan. Scooping up the case, she turned away from the bar and slipped into the crowd. He was right behind her—and right behind them were the Russians. He heard the commotion of them bulling their way through the people packing the room.

Quick on her feet, his girl made it to the balcony five yards ahead of him. In the few extra seconds it took him to get outside, she had already covered the open ground to the broad, stone staircase and was halfway to the first landing, darting her way through people heading upstairs to dine. At midnight, the restaurant would still be busy, and there was a good chance they could slip onto the fire escape before the Russians spotted them.

He caught her on the second landing, and as unobtrusively as possible, the two of them breezed past the hostess and crossed through the maze of tables and diners, heading to the north wall of the building. When they reached the fire escape, Lani quickly stepped over the side, onto the top rung, and started down. He followed, damned impressed that they'd shaken the bad guys.

But then someone swore and she stopped.

"Oh, excuse me," she said between a rapid-fire stream of angry Spanish. "I'm sorry, oh . . . excuse me."

What in the hell was going on, he wondered, trying to look below him. He couldn't see much, staring down into darkness, but she at least started moving again, even though she was still murmuring apologies and someone else was still swearing. A few more rungs down, when he reached the first landing, the situation became crystal clear. Anywhere else in the world, a metal ladder bolted to the side of a building and occasionally interspersed with small metal landings was called a fire escape. In Casco Viejo on a Friday night fueled by *seco con leche* and rum, it was called Lover's Lane.

Clothing was coming off here and there, a jacket, a scarf, a shoe, and buttons were coming undone on every landing all the way to the street.

So much for the afternoon he'd spent planning escape routes. He shrugged out of his too-damn-easy-to-spot white suit jacket and left it hanging on the railing with the other folks' clothes.

When they reached the second landing, someone from above shouted down in thick, Russian-accented Spanish, "*Alto!*" Stop!

Not very damn likely, Jack thought. Some of these folks were past the "stopping" part of the evening. Except he stopped, and Lani stopped, and in the instant of silence between the shouted command and the torrent of verbal abuse directed back up from the people crowding the fire escape, he had a brilliantly tactical idea—camouflage.

Pulling her close, he wrapped her zebra-striped curves in his arms and pressed her up against the building.

Instinct more than brains brought his mouth down on hers, and pure, unadulterated pleasure, sweet and intense, kept it there, moment after lush, sensual moment as her lips parted, welcoming him inside, and so it would have gone, an endless kiss into something more, with her hot body pressed up against his, if the Russians had left.

They did not.

Over the side they came, pushing and shouting for the lovers to get out of their way.

He obliged, pushing Lani ahead of him down the last rungs of the fire escape. Back on the ground, he took her hand in his, and they ran down the nearest alley. In less than a block, they'd left the elegant and brightly lit world of Las Palmas behind and entered the maze of cobblestone streets and narrow walkways that made up the barrio section of the historic old town. He held to a northwest course, making for one of the main streets where they could catch a taxi to the embassy.

The music coming from the hotel's bar grew fainter with every step they took, giving him ample opportunity to silently wonder what in the ever-loving world had he be thinking? He'd manhandled a C.I.A. agent, kissed a spy, ran his hands up the side of her amazing curves and loved every second of it. And in the middle of a rocky escape, way too much of his brain was wondering how to do it again.

The sound of a gunshot zipping down the alley cleared all that nonsense out of his mind in a nano-second. He shoved his shoulder hard against the first wooden door he saw, wrenching the door handle at the same time, and the two of them burst into the overgrown courtyard of an abandoned house.

One thing he really liked about working with her, besides the rare opportunity to kiss the stuffing out of her, was that the two of them thought a lot alike. If this was going to turn into a shoot-out, they needed cover, which she spotted the same time he did, a set of large iron doors hanging half open on the ground floor that must have served as the home's service entrance. She all but dove inside, with him right behind her, almost on top of her, with another shot whacking into the door behind them.

"Cripes!" she swore, breathing hard, her face dirt-streaked, her dress ruined. She was low to the ground, crouched behind the door, looking out the door with a semi-auto pistol in her hands that looked to be .45 caliber—his favorite.

"We've got two problems," he said, his gaze quartering the part of the courtyard he could see without exposing himself. He could tell she was doing the same over on her side.

"The Russians and the cops," she said.

"Exactly." Neither of them wanted to explain their situation to the Panamanian government, local or otherwise. "There's got to be a door that opens onto the street, and we're less than a block off the sea wall. If we can get to the water, we can get to a boat."

"You're thinking like a SEAL."

He almost grinned. "Sweetheart, I *am* a SEAL."

Another shot hit the iron door, and he aimed for the muzzle flash, squeezing off a round that hit something that grunted and moaned.

"Down by one," she said, then fired. "Make that two."

Yeah, he'd heard something else collapse out there with a groan, but there was still a lot of rustling and stumbling going on in the courtyard.

"I think there are more than just the three guys we saw in the Las Palmas," he said.

"I agree. We need to move out, if we're going to get out."

God, they were good together.

"I'll lay down some fire, try to hold their attention

back here while you go out the front."

"I'll meet you at the sea wall." Once again, there was no debate. She took the plan and ran with it, literally, and after a moment's hesitation at the front door to check out the street, she disappeared into the darkness.

He fired a couple more rounds into the courtyard to give the Russians something to think about, and followed her out. They were going to make it.

Then he heard a shot.

Lani heard it, too.

Worse, she'd felt it burn a path across her shoulder. Halfway over the sea wall, she dropped like a stone onto the beach, shocked into losing her grip. She'd never been shot before, and the pain was disorientating. She tried to catch her breath and check herself out, and cursed herself for losing her gun. Before she'd even begun to think straight, let alone decide if she'd done more damage to herself by falling than by getting shot, Jack was there by her side, grim-faced and serious.

"Lani?"

"Flipper?" Okay, she wasn't dying, and a few tentative moves convinced her she hadn't broken anything. "Help me up."

"You're bleeding. Where are you hurt?" His voice was smooth and calm, and just hearing it helped sooth her jangled nerves. He was with her, and they were going to make it out of here—*Yes, ma'am, I can take care of you, one hundred percent guaranteed.*

"My right shoulder."

He looked at the wound and swore softly under his breath. "You're just skinned, babe, but I'm going to carry you."

"Good idea." It was going to take more time than they had for her to get steady on her feet, a fact proved by the shot fired from above. It hit the water, ten feet out, but was still way too damn close.

He turned and raised his pistol in one smooth move, aiming a precise shot toward the top of the wall, and a body came over the side, landing in the sand with a deathly thud.

"Change in plans," he said, kicking off his shoes and stripping off his slacks. "We're heading out to sea."

Another good idea, really, but Lani didn't see a boat anywhere close to where they were beached. Then she did see some boats, a lot of boats, moored at the *Muelle Fiscal* wharf, but the wharf was a long way away.

"How far can you swim?" She thought it was a question worth asking, especially as how he'd already picked her up and was carrying her out into the water.

"Miles," he assured her.

"Yes, but how far can you swim with me?" With the Pacific Ocean lapping at her butt, that was the sticking point.

He just grinned and kissed the tip of her nose as they sunk into the water and he turned her over onto her back. "Even farther," he said.

"The saltwater hurts like hell." And it did, burning like a brand where the bullet had sliced her skin open. For a moment, all she wanted was *out* of the water, and she started to panic.

But his voice came to her, steady as a rock. "I was born in Alabama, in the northern part of the state, and when I was five, my folks packed us all up, my two brothers, one sister, and me and we moved over to Louisiana. Now there's a great state."

Stroke after stroke, they headed into deeper water on a course that would take them to the wharf, where - in between telling her his life story - he informed her they would "borrow" a boat.

He never faltered, not once, not for an instant, but she

did. By the time he got her into one of the motorized canoes the locals called *piraguas,* she felt half dead, feverish, and like she might not make it. But he knew better.

"You're doing great, Lani. Just hang in there. We're almost home. Everything is going to be okay."

Home was the U.S. Embassy. Across the bay, she could see the lights of central Panama City, and as they came up to the Balboa Monument, she knew he was right. Home wasn't very far away.

Slowly, with effort, she brought her hand up to the bodice of her dress and felt the silver cigarette case still secure in the secret pocket.

Yes, she thought. Everything was going to be okay.

EPILOGUE

Four months later, somewhere in Louisiana

"Hey, babe, you want to hand me that bait can?" she asked.

Fishing had been his idea. Jack would be the first to admit it, but who in the world would have guessed his secret agent girlfriend would take to it like a duck to water?

Not him, that was for damn sure, or he might have held off for a few years.

Whether she was after largemouth bass, crappie, or a mess of bream and shellcracker for supper, Little Miss Blondie left his bed way too damn early every morning to get down to the lake and start casting her line.

From where he was stretched out on the dock, he rolled over and looked in the white plastic bucket she'd brought down. The water was murky in the bucket.

"What have you got in here?"

"Ditch shrimp."

"You go, girl," he said around a yawn, pushing the bait bucket in her direction.

He was on leave, and she was still on hiatus, and hiatus looked good on her, almost as good as her Daisy Duke cut-offs and bikini top. Barefoot and suntanned, her hair had gotten long enough for a little ponytail in back, and he knew she liked sporting one around.

He liked sporting her around, taking her down to the nearest backwater roadhouse for crawfish and zydeco, and every night, bringing her back to their cabin in the swamp oak and tupelo forest, where he made love to her by the light of a southern moon.

Down on the end of the dock, she got a bite, her cane pole dipping toward the water, and with a dimpled smile and a short laugh, she pulled the fish in and got busy baiting another shrimp on her line. From this angle, he could see the scar across her shoulder from the night she'd been shot. She thought it made her look tough.

He thought she *was* tough.

"What did you get?" he asked, more to be polite than any actual interest. It was too early in the morning to be interested in fish.

"Bluegill." She looked up with the smile still on her face.

God, she was beautiful. No wonder he loved her. The truth had been staring him down for weeks. Smart, funny, gorgeous women were hard to find, but he'd done it, and he wasn't going to let her go.

He wasn't going to rush things, though. He wanted to give her plenty of time to figure out she was crazy about him, too. So he'd gotten her something special to let her know how he felt. This morning's phone call had cinched it for him.

"I heard from a friend of mine this morning, the guy whose house I was staying in while I was stationed in Panama."

"J.T. Chronopolous, right?" She threw her line back in, casting it into the weed beds lining the bank.

"Yep. Seems he and this group of guys he works with out of a place called Steele Street in Denver tracked down a shipping container full of stolen shoulder-launched surface to air missiles at a port in Yemen."

That got her attention.

She turned to face him so quickly, she almost dropped her pole.

"They found the Stingers?"

"And the Mistrals and the Russian SA-18s." There had been doubts. The encryption on the cigarette case hadn't been as definitive as Nikolayevich had promised. "It's all thanks to you, babe. You saved a lot of lives."

She was beaming, the sunlight caressing her skin and turning it that peachy golden color that made her look good enough to eat. "They found the SAMs."

Oh, yeah. He was in love.

Pushing himself upright, he rolled to his feet and padded down to her end of the dock just to drop down next to her and take her in his arms. She snuggled in close, and he kissed the top of her head. She was warm, and he was in love, and the time was right for the box in his pocket.

"J.T. has a sister-in-law who's an artist, and I had her design and make up something for you." He reached into the pocket of his shorts.

Lani leaned a little ways back, and he opened the box between them. Nestled inside was a necklace, a silver chain with three charms hanging from the middle, two in gold and one in silver.

"Oh, Jack," she whispered, reaching out to take the necklace and hold it in her hand. "It's beautiful, but what . . ."

She was a smart girl, she'd recognize the charms in a minute.

It took less than that.

"Missiles?" She looked up, her expression a fascinating mix of confusion and delight. "You had somebody design little missiles for me?"

He just grinned. Yes, he was the man who knew how to deliver.

"Ohmigosh." A rapturous smile spread across her face.

"This is so awesome."

"One of a kind, sweetheart. Just like you. But a couple of the girls down at Steele Street—"

"The place in Denver," she clarified.

"Yes. They liked your necklace so much, they'd like to have a couple more made. I told them I would check with you. What do you think? Would you mind if Skeeter and Red Dog had necklaces like yours?"

Her eyes widened a little. "I think any woman who would wear missiles on a chain ought to have exactly what she wants. And Skeeter? Red Dog? Cripes, babe, do names even get cooler than that?"

"They're cool, all right. Cool like you." He reached over and took the necklace out of her hand and clasped it around her neck. "Maybe you'll get to meet them someday."

"I'd like that." She looked down and ran the tips of her fingers over the three charms.

"Yeah, I think you would." He leaned in closer and kissed her cheek, and her forehead, and the tip of her nose. "Can we go back to bed, now. Dawn is long gone, thank God, and the fish won't start biting again until noon."

"But, sweetie-pie, it's a gorgeous day out here. What in the world are we going to do in bed?"

His grin broadened. Right, he thought. Like that was a mystery.

In answer, he scooped her up into his arms and started back up the dock. "Oh, I'm guessing we'll figure something out."

She laughed and leaned in close to whisper in his ear. "You know I love you, Flipper."

Yeah, he knew, and my, oh, my, wasn't it really just a damn fine day.

About the Author

TARA JANZEN is the New York Times and Nationally Bestselling Author of eleven Steele Street novels and one Steele Street novella, thirteen Loveswepts, a medieval fantasy trilogy beginning with *The Chalice and The Blade*, and the stand-alone adventure romance *River of Eden*. She has won numerous awards from Romantic Times and a RITA award.

For Exclusive Content sign up for
Tara's Newsletter at:
www.tarajanzen.com
and follow Tara at:

www.facebook.com/tarajanzenauthor

www.instagram.com/tarajanzenauthor/?hl=en

www.bookbub.com/authors/tara-janzen

See you there!

TJ xoxo

Want More...?

IS THIS YOUR FIRST VISIT TO STEELE STREET?
Then Don't Miss

CRAZY HOT
and
CRAZY COOL

Made in the USA
Monee, IL
16 November 2021